The Last Present

The Last Present

WENDY MASS

SCHOLASTIC INC.

A heartfelt thank-you to everyone at Scholastic who lovingly helped bring Willow Falls to life, and to the amazing, inspiring, wonderful readers who came for a visit and never left. You guys are the BEST.

"In every moment something sacred is at stake."
— Rabbi Abraham Joshua Heschel

Prologue
Ten Years Ago

When you've drawn breath for nearly a hundred years, not much surprises you. So when Angelina D'Angelo stepped into the Willow Falls birthing center that hot July day, she didn't expect anything out of the ordinary. She figured she'd be in and out in ten minutes, tops.

But the elevator was broken and she had to take the stairs two flights up. Then a new guard kept asking to see the badge she'd forgotten to affix to her green nurse's outfit. She'd been coming here at least once a week for decades and had gotten used to no one stopping her. A bit rattled, she took a good five minutes to sort through all the badges in her pocket before she found the right one.

She quickened her pace toward the nursery. The clock above the door showed three till noon. She still had time. A quick scan of the room led her to the baby, bundled tight in pink. GRACE ALYSA KELLY, the note card on her bassinet read. GIRL. TIME OF BIRTH: 11 A.M. WEIGHT: 6 POUNDS, 4 OUNCES. A little thing she was. And yet so much depended on her.

With an ease that came from having done this many times before, she scooped the baby into her arms. Bending close, she began to murmur the words that would keep the baby safe.

They poured from her mouth like honey, making the air thick and sweet. The duck-shaped birthmark on Angelina's cheek wiggled as she spoke, but the baby's eyes were too unfocused to be entertained by it.

Knock! Knock!

Angelina looked up in surprise, the words tangling on her tongue. A boy no more than three years old stood at the nursery window, jumping up and down and rapping on the glass wall. She glanced at the clock. 11:59. She bent her head again to continue. Now where was she?

"Grace!" the boy shouted joyfully. "I'm your big brother!"

Angelina scowled. "Hush, Connor!" she scolded in as loud a voice as she dared. "You'll wake all the babies!"

The boy continued waving and stomping, not questioning why she would know his name. Where were his parents? She turned her back on him and resumed her benediction. But wait, had she said this part already? Her heart fluttered with an unfamiliar feeling. Fear.

Thirty seconds left.

Knock! Knock!

She didn't turn to look. A drop of sweat slid down her forehead. Angelina couldn't remember the last time anything had made her sweat. Couldn't someone make that boy go away?

The door to the nursery pushed open and one of the young nurses whose name she never bothered to learn strolled in. "Time to bring that one to her mother for feeding."

Angelina didn't have to check the clock to know she had run out of time.

"Do you want me to bring her?" the young nurse asked. "You look like you could use a rest."

Without a word, Angelina placed the baby in the woman's waiting arms. Then she straightened up, threw a withering look at the boy still banging on the window, and left the nursery. She would have to wait a full year to try again. She couldn't fail twice. Not with this baby. Grace was special.

And it was up to Angelina D'Angelo to keep everyone else in Willow Falls from knowing it.

Chapter One
Amanda

Two years ago I didn't believe in anything I couldn't see with my own eyes. Then Angelina D'Angelo, the oldest woman in Willow Falls, came into my life and turned it upside down. Now she's about to do it again. I'd be freaking out more if I didn't have Leo beside me. Well, behind me in the backseat of Ray's old car, but close enough.

Since Leo and I have each other, we've always tried to be there for anyone else who Angelina has decided to "help." For the past four weeks it's been Tara, who was sent here to live with her aunt and uncle and cousin for the summer as punishment for trying to steal her middle school principal's goat. She doesn't think we know the reason she was expelled from school, but this is a small town. People talk. Angelina assigned Tara to hunt down thirteen random objects that turned out not to be so random after all. It ended yesterday when Angelina tricked her into putting on a production of *Fiddler on the Roof* and we all had to be in it. I have three blisters on my feet from the boots I had to wear. I'm still not sure how this helped Tara, but when I saw her this morning she was happier than I'd ever seen her, so something big must have happened after the play.

Last year Angelina set her sights on Rory, who had made a list of everything she'd be able to do when she turned twelve. Angelina apparently decided there were no lessons to be learned by getting everything you thought you wanted. Poor Rory spent months dealing with one crazy situation after another, most of them caught on film by the movie crew at our school! She was a good sport about it all, though, much better than I would have been! The whole town will probably be at the premiere of the movie tonight, which is going to be awesome. I hope that whatever Angelina has planned for me and Leo, we'll still get to go.

Even though we've known for a full year that this day would come, I'm still sort of stunned that it's happening. I'm sure Rory and Tara are worried about us after we ran off and left them back at David's bar mitzvah without an explanation. Leo, Rory, Tara, and I are the only ones who know that Angelina has special powers. David doesn't know, even though he spent the last few weeks helping Tara with her list, and he starred in the play, too, all while practicing for his bar mitzvah. That's just how it is with Angelina: You keep her secrets and she keeps yours. Judging from the way David looks at Tara when he doesn't think anyone's watching, he'd do practically anything for her, whether or not he knows the reason why.

I glance over my shoulder at Leo, who is watching downtown disappear through his window. His face is calm, but I know his thoughts are on Grace, and on what we're going to find when we arrive at the hospital. Whatever is in store for us, we will handle it together. We're a good team. And if it wasn't for Angelina, we may never have become best friends again. Our experience two years ago bonded us together forever. In appreciation, I'll do whatever she wants. I've definitely proved this by agreeing not to talk directly to Leo for the past year. Now *that's* dedication. It's one thing not talking to your best friend when you're in a fight and don't want to. It's another thing entirely when all you want to hear is his voice and you can't. This time we're more prepared. We're not only two years older, we're two years wiser. We know that sometimes the most important things are the ones you can't see.

"Seriously, Ray," Leo complains from the backseat, his calm broken. "If you were driving any slower, we'd be going backward." David's service had been at Apple Grove, where he chanted and sang surrounded by all the baby apple trees we planted last year in an effort to get the place back to its past glory. Unfortunately, Apple Grove is as far from the hospital as you can get and still be a part of Willow Falls.

"I know this car must be older than you are," Leo continues, "but have you suddenly turned into a little old lady? Pedal to the metal, dude."

"Don't crack a fruity, mate," Ray says in his twangy Australian accent. "I'm going as fast as I can."

Leo kicks the seat. "Are you? Are you really?"

"Aye, little mate. Don't grizzle. You could always ask someone else to drive you places, you know."

We really can't. Ray works for Tara's uncle at their house, so he's always around. And he doesn't ask too many questions. Usually I get shy in front of him because he's so cute. Like, Australian rock star cute with his tan and his long blond hair and his broad shoulders and that accent. But since I still can't talk directly to Leo until Angelina says it's okay, I need to say something to someone or I just might burst from nerves. So I turn to Ray. "*Crack a fruity? Grizzle?* What does that even mean? And how come when you say things, it always sounds like you're asking a question even when you're not?"

Ray chuckles. "That's an Aussie trait. We all sound like that. *Crack a fruity* means go crazy. To *grizzle* is to complain. Your boyfriend back there is doing both. Anyone want to tell me why you two are all worked up?"

My first instinct is to argue that Leo isn't my boyfriend. But I've learned to let the comment pass. People have been whispering about us for years, and now that we're thirteen it's gotten worse. They'll believe whatever they want anyway. "I told you already. Connor's sister, Grace, was taken to the hospital this morning and we need to check on her. It happened right before David's bar mitzvah started, but we didn't find out until after the service."

Ray finally speeds up as we leave the downtown shopping area behind. "Amanda, Amanda, Amanda," he says, pronouncing it like *em-eye-ndeh*. "I like Grace, too. She's a funny kid and was fab in our production of *Fiddler on the Roof* yesterday. But there's more going on here than your concern over the well-being of a girl ya hardly know." He points to the blackboard hanging around my neck, which Leo and I have used for the past year to communicate with each other. "A lot more going on."

He's right, of course. We barely know Grace. Her older brother, Connor, is David's best friend, but even though we've gotten to know David very well this last year, all we know about Connor is that he plays a lot of video games, smiles easily, wants to be an inventor like Tara's uncle when he grows up, and is a really good friend to David. We still don't know why or how we're involved in whatever happened that sent Grace to the hospital. But Leo and I have the power to make something happen today that nobody else can — we just don't know what that is. Stalling, I say, "Tara was right. You really *can* speak with normal words if you want to."

He grunts in reply. I watch him drive out of the corner of my eye, debating what to say. I do kind of like the idea of an adult knowing what's going on, in case something happens to us. And even though Ray's car makes scary clanging noises and doesn't go very fast, he's always willing to drive us places. And he did direct a whole play with only two weeks' notice just because we asked him to.

My phone dings with a text. I pull it out of my bag. It's from Leo.

AFTER ALL HE DID FOR TARA THIS SUMMER, I THINK WE CAN TRUST HIM. HE DIDN'T HAVE TO HELP HER FIND THAT STUFF FOR HER LIST OR DIRECT THE PLAY, AND ONCE ANGELINA TELLS US WHAT'S GOING ON, WE MIGHT NEED SOMEONE WHO CAN DRIVE US PLACES. OUR PARENTS WOULD ASK WAY TOO MANY QUESTIONS.

Sometimes with Leo it's like we share a brain.

Ray glances over at my phone. "Hope you got the unlimited plan. Tara told me you two haven't spoken to each other face-to-face for almost a year."

"Actually, as of today it's *exactly* a year." I take a deep breath. "If I answer your question from before, will you promise not to tell anyone?"

"Scout's honor," he promises.

"You were a Boy Scout?" Leo calls from the back.

"Made it all the way to Rover Scout," Ray says proudly.

Leo chuckles. "Is that like an Eagle Scout? You must have been very popular in high school."

"Spot on, mate."

"Can we focus, please?" I ask, spitting out the nail I just bit off. It sticks to the dashboard.

Ray casts me a look. "Charming."

I flick the nail off the dash. "Sorry, bad habit I just picked up." I waffle for a second, unsure how much to tell him. I glance back at Leo, who tilts his head and nods, urging me on. Over the past year we've learned to read each other's facial expressions so well that we can carry on full conversations that way. It's amazing how much you can communicate using your eyes, mouth, neck, and shoulders.

I take a deep breath. "I know this is going to sound crazy, but Leo and I found out two years ago that time stops for us after a year of not talking. It's too complicated to explain the whole story about why it happens, but it has something to do with our ancestors. We haven't spoken to each other face-to-face since last July fourteenth. Exactly a year ago today." Now that I've said it out loud, it feels right. It feels like he's supposed to know.

Ray keeps his eyes on the road. He makes the final turn toward the hospital and says, "If you didn't want to tell me, you could have just said so."

"She's telling the truth," Leo says, leaning forward and grasping the back of Ray's seat. "We've been waiting all year for this day. We have no idea what's supposed to happen. First we thought it had to do with David because of his bar mitzvah. Like maybe something would go wrong that we needed to fix. But nothing went wrong. Then we thought maybe it had to do with Tara, but we could tell this morning that something big had happened to her after the play last night, and by this morning, she didn't need us anymore. Then, after David's bar mitzvah service, we found out that Grace's parents had to rush her to the hospital. Once we heard that it's her tenth birthday, we knew for sure that whatever it is we're supposed to do, Grace is involved somehow. Birthdays are a really big deal with Angelina."

Ray pulls to a stop in front of the main entrance to the hospital. He turns to face us. "Angelina, the short old lady who works all around town? The one in the front row at *Fiddler* yesterday?"

We both nod.

Ray pulls a wad of bills out of his front pocket. "She gave me a hundred bucks after the play ended. Said I'd need it for gas money this week. I figured she'd gone loony, but before I could give it back, someone else stopped to congratulate me on directing the play and when I turned around again, she'd split."

Leo and I exchange a grin. His story confirms that we were definitely supposed to tell him. "Well, Ray, now you know the mystery that is Angelina D'Angelo."

"We've got to get inside," Leo says, opening his door with a loud creak.

I untangle the seat belt from my blackboard. I definitely won't miss having this thing around my neck every time Leo and I are together.

After one last stare at the money in his palm, Ray tucks it away and says, "I can't just leave you here."

"That's really nice of you," I tell him, "but we don't know how long we'll be."

"Or even if today will be today when we come back out," Leo says, sticking his head into my window. "Today could be today for us and tomorrow for you. Or next week!"

Ray scratches his head. "Huh?"

"Exactly," I say, pushing my door open.

"I'll take my chances that your today and my today will be the same when you come back." Ray starts the car. "I'll be in the parking lot when you come out."

If we come out. I thank him, take a deep breath, and run after Leo. Whether or not Ray fully believes us, I'm glad he's out there.

The first person I see when I step through the large sliding glass door is Connor's dad. I recognize him from the play last night. He was filming the whole thing with a camera he set up on a tripod in front of the stage. Now he's fighting with a coffee machine in the lobby of the Willow Falls Hospital. Judging by his mangled Styrofoam cup, I'd say the machine is winning.

"Mr. Kelly!" Leo says, hurrying over to him. "Is Grace all right? I'm Leo, and this is Amanda. We're friends of Connor's. We were all in the play together last night? We figured since David couldn't be here for Connor, that we'd come instead."

We hadn't actually discussed how to explain our visit. Guess his explanation is as good as any. Leo is good at lying while not really lying at the same time.

Mr. Kelly looks down at us from his considerable height. His bloodshot eyes are almost as red as his hair. "I remember you," he says, tossing his torn coffee cup into the trash. He looks back and forth between us. "What's with the blackboards? Some fashion trend I've missed?"

"Long story," I tell him.

"We'll be throwing them out very soon," Leo adds. "Hopefully."

Mr. Kelly tries in vain to get more coffee with another cup, but this time a chunk of Styrofoam comes off in his hands and it almost spills all over him. He grunts in frustration. "So you came here to see Connor? Grace is the one we brought in."

"Yes, of course we're here for Grace, too," I assure him. "She and I got pretty close during rehearsals." This isn't exactly true, but she did play my daughter. "In fact, this morning at the bar mitzvah she called me Mommy."

"That sounds like Grace." His mouth curves up a bit and twitches, as though it's currently unable to make a real smile.

"So what happened?" Leo presses. "Did she get sick?"

"Not exactly," he says. "She seems to be in shock. Or something like it. The doctors are afraid she's going catatonic." His voice breaks. "That means her brain can't send messages to her body. She's not talking or moving."

My stomach twists. Leo turns pale. I don't know what I'd expected, maybe a weird strain of the flu, or a stomach virus. But not this.

"Come," he says, waving for us to follow. "See for yourself."

As we wait for the elevator, Leo says, "She seemed perfectly fine at the play last night. Running around, having fun like normal."

"It struck very suddenly," Mr. Kelly says. "Just a few hours ago she was so excited to go to the bar mitzvah. She couldn't wait to play with her brother's friends." He stops talking while a family exits the elevator and we step on. He presses the button for the third floor. An older couple carrying pink balloons and flowers slip in right before the door closes. The woman — who I quickly deduce is a new grandmother — uses her elbow to push the button for the floor marked BIRTHING CENTER. "Our daughter just had a baby," they gush. We try to smile for them, but like Mr. Kelly before, it's hard to make our mouths go that way.

The couple gets out on the second floor and Mr. Kelly continues his story. "So we arrived at Apple Grove early this morning. Connor needed to set up the video feed to allow David's father to watch the service." He pauses. "I hope that worked out all right?"

We nod. "It worked perfectly," I tell him. "It was like David's father was in the field with us."

"It was Connor's idea in the first place," Leo adds. "He worked out the whole thing with the clinic where David's dad lives."

"He gets his technical skills from me," Mr. Kelly says, pride evident in his voice. Then his expression saddens. "When Phil — that's David's dad — first got sick, Mrs. Kelly and I used to drive David and his mother up to see him at the clinic. Phil could still crack jokes, and could even get around a bit on his own. But once his condition worsened, they stopped asking us to come."

Neither of us says anything. David's never spoken much about his dad, at least not to me. I know his condition is permanent, and hereditary, which means that David might get sick one day, too. Mr. Kelly shakes his head as though shaking off the sad memories before picking up his story. "So Connor finishes setting up and we're about to take our seats when Grace starts breathing heavily, gasping almost. We thought maybe she was having an allergic reaction to a bee sting or something, but we couldn't find any sign of it. At first she could still talk. In fact, all she was doing was talking. But it wasn't making any sense. She kept talking about strings in the sky. She kept saying what sounded like 'Willow Falls is a blanket.'"

"'Willow Falls is a blanket'?" Leo repeats as we step out of the elevator and turn down a long hallway. "What does that mean?"

"We have no idea. Then, just as suddenly, she stopped speaking at all. She didn't appear to hear us, either. I carried her back to the car and brought her straight here." He doesn't talk after that, just strides quickly past rows of closed doors. The halls have that cleaning solution smell to them, which I guess is better than a lot of other smells a hospital could have.

When we get to Grace's room, all I can see at first is a metal bed completely surrounded by doctors with white coats and clipboards. In the absence of any chairs, Mrs. Kelly is sitting on a window seat that looks out onto the parking lot. Her face is white and she keeps clenching and unclenching her hands. I don't see Connor. He's such a good brother, he's probably in the gift shop getting Grace some balloons.

Everyone is talking at once. From what I can make out, the doctors are debating various solutions. I hear words like *benzodiazepine treatment, intravenous fluids, shock therapy*. My heart beats faster. Those don't sound fun. Finally a gray-haired doctor tells everyone that the best thing to do right now is to make sure she's comfortable and not dehydrated. One by one, the doctors and nurses trail out into the hall. I hear one of the doctors mutter, "Never seen anything like it. Not in Willow Falls."

Mr. Kelly hurries in and we follow behind. I stop short when I see Grace. She is lying on top of the covers, her small body taking up very little space on the bed. She's still wearing the pretty striped dress she wore to the bar mitzvah. She should be on her way to the community center right now with the rest of David's guests to dance and celebrate, not stuck here with doctors poking and prodding her. Her mother had braided her long red hair for the party and the braids are now neatly draped over her shoulders. Her bright blue eyes are wide open. Almost *too* wide. She is unmoving, her face frozen in place like a Halloween mask. As someone who has become an expert in reading facial expressions, I can easily recognize the one on her face now.

It's *amazement*.

Chapter Two

I scribble the word on my blackboard and hold it up to Leo. He nods, then writes, *I was going to say awe. And also confusion.*

I nod in agreement. He takes my hand and squeezes it. My pulse quickens whenever he does that. I squeeze back, grateful as always that he's here with me. We step closer to the bed. I don't see pain anywhere on Grace's face, which is a great relief. I can't help but wonder what her last conscious thought was before she froze. I'm not sure what her parents see when they look at her. Judging from their own expressions of worry and fear, they must not see what we see. Or maybe it doesn't matter to them. They just want their daughter back.

"Mr. and Mrs. Kelly?" a woman asks from behind us. Her voice is all business. "Please take a few moments to visit the main office. They need to go over hospital procedures, sign paperwork. Insurance, visiting hours, that sort of thing."

I almost don't look away from the bed. But something about that nurse's voice sounds familiar. So does the ever so slight smell of apples that wafts through the room. Leo and I turn in unison.

Angelina! She is no longer wearing the dress I saw her in at the bar mitzvah service, or the purple scarf. Instead, she has on a green nurse's uniform, complete with an official-looking badge and sneakers almost as white as her hair. I wonder where she got the outfit. We were clearly right to come here. Not that I'd really doubted it, but seeing her is nice confirmation. For some reason though, I find myself a little annoyed. She could have told us where to come instead of making us guess. Even when she needs our help, she's secretive. I look at her expectantly. She looks right past me.

"We'll stay here with Grace," Leo offers. Grace's parents exchange a look that says they're not sure about leaving her with two kids they barely know.

"I'll be here as well," Angelina says, straightening her uniform. "I'll come get you immediately if there are any changes to her vital signs."

"All right," Mrs. Kelly says with a concerned glance at the bed. She picks up her pocketbook and squeezes me on the shoulder as she heads to the door. I feel my anger at Angelina drain away a bit.

"And you might want to tell someone the coffee machine in the lobby is broken," Mr. Kelly adds.

"I'll get right on that," Angelina replies, closing the door behind them.

I put my hands on my hips. "So you're pretending to be a nurse now?"

She shrugs. "I've been a nurse for a long, long time."

"So let's see," Leo says, ticking off on his fingers, "that makes you a nurse, a school bus driver, the owner of Angelina's

Sweet Repeats and Collectibles, the caretaker of the Willow Falls Historical Society, a ticket taker at the Willow Falls Reservoir where you've been known to rescue people from drainpipes, a server in the school cafeteria, and one time you worked at the paint-your-own-pottery store where Amanda and I had our fifth birthday party. That's seven jobs. Did I miss any?"

"You missed plenty," she snaps. "I like to stay busy." She glances over at Grace and a shadow crosses her face.

I put my hand on Angelina's arm. "Today's the day, Angelina. You obviously knew this would happen to Grace. It would have been nice to warn us, but I guess then you wouldn't be you. Tell us what to do. Tell us how to fix it."

"If only it were that simple," she says, sitting down on the end of the bed. There's plenty of room, since Grace fills only the top half.

"Is it all right to talk in front of her?" Leo asks, gesturing toward Grace. "I feel kind of weird about it."

"She can't hear us," Angelina says, shaking her head. "She's in her own world now and we can't reach her."

Leo gives the wide-eyed Grace one last uncertain look before facing Angelina. "Is this like last time, when we wake up tomorrow, it will be today again? Then, somehow, Amanda and I will be able to prevent this from happening to Grace? That's your plan, right?"

To my surprise, Angelina shakes her head. "It will be different this time. When you wake up tomorrow, it will be tomorrow, same as for everyone. But for the next ten days, the two of you will be able to travel back to today, only a different year each time."

I let her words sink in, trying to absorb what they mean.

Leo scratches his head. "Huh?"

"*Huh* is not a word," she says. "Honestly! How do young people today expect to make it in the world without using real words? It's all *omg* and *brb* and *lol* and —"

"Angelina!" we cry. I look quickly at Grace to see if we'd disturbed her, or better yet, woken her up. Nope. No change. It's like she's a statue in the bed. Or a doll.

Angelina is still for a minute. Then she whispers, "This is all my fault."

Our eyebrows shoot up. Angelina admitting any wrongdoing? Unheard of! I want her to explain what she meant about traveling back in time, which is very different from being stuck in time like before, but I can't pass up the chance to hear her admit to something being her fault. She stands up and begins to pace, her white rubber sneakers squeaking unpleasantly. "You know how kids don't get sick very often in Willow Falls?" she finally says. "Or at least not seriously ill?"

"Yeah," Leo replies. "I mean, *yes*."

"Did you ever wonder why?"

We both shake our heads. I never really thought about it before.

"Well, it's because every time a baby is born, it's my job to come to the birthing center and seal them off from harm within an hour of their birth."

"Seal them off from harm?" I repeat. "What does that mean?"

She waves me off with her hand. "I don't expect you to understand. I bestow a benediction upon them. It took years to get it just right, even with all my special abilities. It's like a blessing. A binding spell. The protection lasts eighteen years. But I made a mess of it with Grace. I was late, her brother distracted me, and I ran out of time."

"Her brother?" I ask. "You mean Connor?"

She nods and her pacing quickens. "He was banging on the nursery window. I kept losing my place. Once I realized I'd failed, I started plotting my next move. I'd have another chance to set things right on her first birthday. All year I worried she would fall ill, a tiny little thing she was, but except for a few months when she wouldn't keep much food down, she made it. I showed up at the Kellys' door, right on time, ready to give Grace the benediction she deserved."

Her pacing slows and her face darkens. "But they wouldn't let me in. They said Grace had just been put down for her nap. Even though I hadn't thought to wear my uniform, I explained I had been the nurse on duty when she was born and it was tradition for us to wish the babies a happy birthday when they turned one."

Leo nods appreciatively. "Quick thinking."

Angelina ignores the compliment. "They finally allowed me inside, although the looks they gave each other let me know they hoped I'd be quick about it. Mrs. Kelly led me to Grace's room, but something stopped me from going in."

"You mean you changed your mind?" I ask.

She shakes her head. "No, I mean something literally stopped me. It was as though an invisible shield barred my way. Until today, I have not been allowed in the same room as Grace on her birthday."

"Where could the shield have come from?" I ask.

"As far as I know," she says grimly, "the only person power-ful enough to erect such a shield is me. I certainly didn't do it on purpose, but perhaps I was punishing myself for my fail-ure on the day of her birth. It had been a mistake simply showing up like that. I needed to think of another way. I needed to work harder. So I spent the following year figuring out how to weave the benediction into her birthday celebration so that it would work without me being there. On her second birthday, when her guests sang to her, they would unknowingly be weaving my spell for me."

She holds up a hand. "And don't even bother to ask me how I could do this. I cannot possibly explain. But this time, too, I was thwarted. Grace was sick with a stomach bug — she often had digestive troubles, which kept her small and vexed me to no end. As a result her party was cancelled, nobody sang 'Happy Birthday' and the spell was never released. By her third birth-day, I had begun to panic. I couldn't fail again."

I glance over at the unmoving Grace. "But you did," I whisper.

"Yes," Angelina says, following my gaze. "I failed again that third year. And every year since. I wove the protective spell in so many different ways — once, it would kick in when she blew out her candles, another time it was the balloons — you get the picture. Each time something went wrong. It was uncanny. My plan never got a chance to work."

"But why couldn't you just tell Grace's parents? I'm sure they would have helped you."

She shakes her head. "No one can know what I do to protect the children. I took a sworn oath."

"But you're telling *us*," Leo points out.

She shrugs. "You already know my secrets."

I put my hands on my hips and purse my lips.

"Maybe not all of them," she admits.

"More like *none* of them," I mutter. After all these years we don't know where Angelina lives, where she came from, why she's in Willow Falls, how or why she does what she does. None of it. "But why is Grace like this now?"

Angelina strides over and reaches toward Grace's head. I think she's going to stroke her hair, but instead she gently lowers her eyelids. It makes Grace look more at peace, and less like she's listening to our every word.

"Her ninth birthday was my last chance," Angelina explains, turning away from the bed. "If I failed, I would not be able to stop whatever was on its way when she turned ten years old." She gestures behind her. "This was the result. Thanks to your great-great-grandparents' curse, the two of you are her only hope now." She checks her watch. "We still have a while before her parents return. I made sure they'd be busy with paperwork."

"What do you want us to do?" I ask.

She points at both of us in turn. "I want you to go back to every one of Grace's birthdays until you are able to fix what went wrong. You will have to succeed three times. Once that happens, Grace will be protected from serious harm for the rest of her childhood, until she turns eighteen. And most important, she will awaken from this state."

"Why three times?" I ask.

She shrugs again. "Who knows? Three is tradition. I don't make the rules."

"Then who does?" Leo asks.

Angelina ignores the question, but her face softens. "I know I'm asking a lot of you. It's not like last time, when the choice wasn't yours to make. After all I've put you through these last few years, I would understand if one or both of you don't want to take the very real risks that go along with altering the past. Time will be moving at the same pace for everyone. The present will continue moving forward, adjusting to the changes you make in the past. Bottom line — whatever you do in the past can and will affect the present. Be very careful to only change what is absolutely necessary to get the job done."

My head is beginning to swim with all these instructions. And I'm hungry, which doesn't help my powers of concentration.

"You'll need to follow my instructions very carefully," she continues. "Impact the lives of those around you as little as possible. This especially applies to people you know, like Grace's family. They cannot discover that you are trying to change their history. You must alter only one thread of the past, lest the whole future unravel with it. I need to hear that you both understand this."

Leo says, "Are you telling us that if we make some really small change in the past, like teaching some kid at Grace's birthday party how to tie her shoes before she would normally have learned, when we get back the world might be totally different? Like maybe we'd have never been born, or we could find ourselves in the middle of a zombie apocalypse, running for our lives?"

She rolls her eyes. "I'd say the risk of that is low. You're not going back in time far enough to infect the world's population with a deadly flesh-craving virus."

"Then I'll take my chances," I tell her. "Leo and I managed not to talk for an entire year in preparation for this day. We're going to see it through, no matter what. And I'm kind of relieved we won't be stuck in the same day again. That was pretty crazy."

"It wasn't all bad," Leo argues. "It had its moments." We share a secret smile. No one will ever know everything that happened on those eleven days except for us.

"I'm still not sure how we're going to be able to make this work," I tell her. "But I'll do whatever I can to help."

"So will I," a boy's voice says. Only the voice doesn't belong to Leo.

The three of us freeze. We slowly turn around to find Connor standing in the doorway, holding hands with a SpongeBob SquarePants balloon. Only one of them is smiling, and it isn't Connor.

Chapter Three

Unlike the SpongeBob balloon my parents got for me on my eleventh birthday, which had limbs made of streamers, this one has fully inflated arms and legs that make him look like a small, oddly-shaped child floating a few inches off the ground. I'm aware this isn't a detail I should be focusing on right now, but I'm afraid to look directly at Connor.

Leo clears his throat. "Um, hi, Connor. Did you, um, hear what we were talking about?"

Connor walks unsteadily into the room, the balloon strolling in beside him. Gone is the boy who flounced across the stage last night singing (badly), with a pillow stuffed under his shirt and a fake beard. Though he's dressed up for the bar mitzvah, he looks like a black-and-white photocopy of that person now. Pale and shaky. Even his red hair has dimmed.

He crosses over to the bed. "I heard Amanda tell the nurse that she wants to help," he says. "I want to help, too. Grace is a really good kid and she doesn't deserve this, whatever it is." His voice cracks. "She's really goofy and much smarter than me and she laughs at my jokes even when they're really bad, which they usually are."

I let out a sigh of relief. He didn't hear us. Angelina keeps her eyes averted from Connor's as she fluffs the pillow behind Grace's head and lifts Grace's wrist to take her pulse.

Now that I can breathe again, I walk over to him. "Whatever we can do, just ask, okay, Connor? We can bring her favorite things; maybe that will help somehow."

He nods and sniffles. "That's a good idea." Then in a whisper he asks, "What if she's in pain?"

"She doesn't look like she's in pain to me," I say truthfully.

"I . . . I guess not," Connor says, studying his sister's face.

"I don't think so, either," Angelina says, speaking for the first time since Connor arrived. "She's not in any danger, don't worry. We will do everything we can to keep her comfortable until she comes around."

A second later the door swings open again. The Kellys barely even notice us in their rush to get to Grace's bedside. We quickly part to let them through. Angelina explains about closing Grace's eyes, and I can see Mrs. Kelly's disappointment that they didn't shut on their own.

"All right," Angelina says, all businesslike again. "Time for visitors to go."

Mrs. Kelly turns to me and Leo. "Did someone drop you off?"

"Our friend Ray is waiting outside," I tell her. "The guy who directed the play? He's going to take us back to David's party."

"I'd like you to join your friends," Mrs. Kelly tells Connor. "David worked very hard for this day and without his father there, well, he should have his best friend. We'll call you with any news."

Connor tries to argue, but Mrs. Kelly holds up her hand. "We'll be fine. Your aunts will be here soon, so we'll have plenty of company."

"Fine," Connor grumbles. "But I'll be back as soon as it's over."

Angelina makes a note on the chart hanging off the end of Grace's bed. Then she says to Connor, "Why don't you say good-bye to your sister while I get these two some volunteer badges." She doesn't wait for his response before ushering us out the door. "We'll meet you in the lobby," Leo calls back to him.

Angelina leads us into an empty waiting room at the far end of the hall, past the elevators. "We don't have much time," she says, reaching into her pocket. She hands me a small spiral notebook. "I recorded my plans for each party in there. It will tell you the exact point in each party where the benediction failed. Once that moment passes, so does your chance to fix it."

I flip open the notebook and immediately recognize Angelina's small, even handwriting. Each page lists where the party was held and what object or action carried the benediction. I read out loud, "Ninth birthday: bowling alley, goody bags, must be distributed. Eighth birthday: beach, balloons, must stay tethered. Seventh birthday —"

"All right, you can study them tonight and prepare your strategy. We still have a lot to go over."

"The premiere is tonight," Leo reminds her.

"The what?"

"The premiere?" he repeats. "For the movie they filmed at our school last year that Amanda and Rory and I were extras in? Starring the world-famous Jake Harrison and Madison Waters? Jake, who's, like, almost dating Rory now?"

She gives him a blank stare, totally uninterested in what was no doubt the most exciting thing to happen in Willow Falls since, well, *ever*.

"As I was saying," she continues, "you'll go over the material so you're as prepared as possible. You will be revisiting each birthday in order from the most recent to the most distant. You will begin tomorrow, at the bowling alley, the location of last year's birthday party. You will need to be there before the party begins. Once you are in place, your great-great-grandfathers' curse will begin and you'll be transported back in time to the same spot."

"I prefer the word *enchantment*, or *spell*," Leo says. "*Curse* sounds so gloom and doom-ish."

"You may call it whatever you like," she snaps, "just do not be late. When your mission is complete, you will return to the place from which you left, and you will be transported back to the present."

I have so many questions, but I start with, "What if we can't stop it from going wrong? Can we keep going back to that same party until we get it right?"

She shakes her head. "You will only be able to visit each day once. Whether you succeed or fail, the following day will bring you to the previous birthday. Remember, you only need to succeed three times. Your journey back in time can end in three days, or in nine. Aim for three."

My stomach growls. I had been too nervous to have breakfast this morning. I really should have grabbed some of those mini–hot dogs at the bar mitzvah.

Worry flits across Leo's face. "What you said before, about

time moving forward here while we're gone? If that's true, then when we go to the past, we'll just disappear from the present. That's something our parents are gonna notice."

"Hmm, I hadn't really considered that." She thinks for a moment, then clicks her tongue. "Well, you'll come up with something."

"Great," we both mutter.

"We need to get back to the bar mitzvah before David gets suspicious," I tell her. "We don't want him to know about Grace until after, so it doesn't ruin his party."

"Hey, when will Amanda and I be able to talk again?" Leo asks.

Angelina pulls two volunteer badges from her pocket. She hands both of them to me. "You can talk now if you want. Just beware of breaking the curse too soon. Do it in the past, and you'll be trapped there."

Leo and I stare at each other, wide-eyed. We can talk again! He gives a single shake of his head and I know exactly what he means. *Not here. When we're alone.* I turn back to Angelina to remind her that the little apple trees, which kept the curse from breaking last time, have now been planted in Apple Grove. But she's gone. Vanished in that way that only she can do.

Leo lifts up his blackboard and scribbles, *How does she do that?*

I won't miss these, I scribble back.

Let's take the stairs, he writes, and points to the sign outside the small room.

I nod. Something about being in a hospital makes the idea of flying down stairs sound really appealing. He grabs my hand

and we run down the whole three flights without stopping. I hold the blackboard to my chest so it doesn't keep smacking me. All I can think is *We can talk! We can talk!* It's like having your birthday present waiting for you at the end of your bed, but going to brush your teeth first.

We meet Connor by the front door. On the way to the parking lot, he asks, "Do you think Ray would mind stopping at my house first? I want to pick up a few things of Grace's to bring back with me, like you suggested."

"I'm sure he wouldn't mind," I say. "He's pretty adaptable."

Ray is leaning against his car door when we arrive. "So, I see today is still today."

Connor raises his eyebrows. "As opposed to next Thursday?"

Ray opens his mouth to answer, but Leo gives him a quick shake of his head. After Connor ducks into the car I whisper to Ray not to say anything about what we told him. I can tell by the way he keeps tapping his fingers on the steering wheel as he drives that he wants to know what happened with Angelina. That will have to wait. Angelina made it very clear that Connor can't find out.

When we get to his house, Connor runs right up to Grace's room and starts sweeping things off her dresser into a small duffel bag. Without turning around he says, "Will you guys grab me some movies for Grace to watch? They're on a shelf in my dad's office at the end of the hall."

"Movies?" I'm not sure what use Grace would have with those when she doesn't seem to be able to see anything around her.

"I read somewhere that watching funny movies when they're in the hospital helps patients heal faster."

"Okay," I tell him, stepping around him as he sweeps Grace's history textbook from last year into the bag, along with a half-eaten candy bar and a used tissue. Pretty sure Grace won't be wanting those, but I don't stop him. Her room looks exactly like you'd expect it to look for a ten-year-old getting ready for a fancy party. Clothes pulled from drawers and off hangers, ripped tights in a ball on the floor, an instant message open on her computer to her friend Bailey, asking if she should wear her hair up or down. Her playbill from the play last night is pinned to her bulletin board. She drew little pink hearts around the edges. Seeing that makes me sad again. I'm sure Grace never imagined she wouldn't be returning to her room tonight. It strikes me that one day all of us will leave a room for the last time and not know it. Not that I think Grace won't be coming back. I can't let myself think that.

Leo nudges me with the edge of his blackboard. His raised eyebrow and the slight creases in the corners of his eyes mean he's asking if I'm okay. I shake myself out of my dark thoughts and nod. We leave Connor and hurry down the hall.

The shelf is more like an entire wall full of shelves. Upon first glance, I can tell about half of the DVDs are movies whose names I recognize, and the other half are home videos, labeled according to event and date. Family trips, dance recitals, soccer practices, first haircuts. Mr. Kelly must have a video camera glued to his face. I start to pull out the DVDs that I think Grace would enjoy, or rather that a normal version of Grace would enjoy.

I've just added a copy of *Shrek* to my growing pile, when Leo pulls out one of the videos and waves it in front of my face.

Connor's and Grace's Birthdays is written across the front in neat black letters. My eyes bug out of my head. I lift my blackboard and chalk, and start writing. I know we can talk now, but I don't want our first words in a year to be about someone else's home movies. *Do you think it will show what happened?* I write.

He scrawls, *One way to find out.* He runs behind the desk, opens the first drawer, and holds up a box of flash drives triumphantly. He writes on his board again and turns it toward me. *Keep Connor away.*

Before I can protest, he's behind Mr. Kelly's desk, booting up his computer. I grab my pile of movies and run out. I can't watch.

Turns out Connor isn't upstairs anymore anyway. I find him down in the kitchen, rummaging through the pantry and stuffing snack bars into his already full duffel bag. He's holding Grace's pillow under one arm. With his suit on he looks like a well-dressed burglar.

"Um, Leo just had to use the bathroom. He'll be right down." Ugh, I hate lying. There's no way to make that one into a lie that isn't really a lie.

A minute later we hear the toilet flush upstairs. Yup, there's that whole sharing-a-brain thing again.

.   .   .   .

As soon as we step foot inside the community center, David breaks away from the dance floor, which has been set up where the bingo tables usually are. He comes bounding up to us, a little sweaty in his fancy bar-mitzvah-boy suit. Happy sweaty, though, not gross sweaty. "Where have you been?" he asks us over the loud music. "Rory and Tara said you had to go do something, but wouldn't tell me what." Before we can reply, he turns to Connor and says, "What's this about a wedding your parents forgot about?"

"They thought I should be here after all," Connor says, putting on a brave smile. "The others are really sorry to miss it, though."

Taking a cue from Connor, I sidestep the truth and say, "We brought your gift!" I hold open my pocketbook to show him the small wrapped box inside. It's been there all day but he doesn't need to know that. The flash drive with the videos that Leo "borrowed" from Mr. Kelly is lying underneath.

David laughs. "You didn't have to miss an hour of the party to get it!" He reaches for it, his fingers grazing the flash drive and causing my heart to skip a beat. Then he holds the box up to his ear and gives it a shake. "It's not a tiny periodic table, right? 'Cause I still have the one you made me when I almost knocked you down in the hallway at school a few years ago."

"Sorry, Bee Boy. You only get one of those per lifetime."

"You mean, sorry, *Hamburglar*," Connor argues.

"Bee Boy!"

"Hamburglar!"

I push him and he laughs for the first time today. Connor and I have never been able to agree on David's nickname. I prefer the one I gave him when he wore a yellow-and-black shirt the day we first met in fifth grade. He had been bumped up to a sixth-grade science class and was nearly in tears about forgetting his homework. Connor would rather play off David's last name, Goldberg, and his favorite food, hamburgers. "Give it up, Red," I say, making up a nickname for him.

"Hey, only my uncle Bill can call me that, Little Drummer Girl."

"*Hamburglar* doesn't even makes sense," I insist. "It's not even a word."

"Yes, it is. It's the giant talking hamburger from the McDonald's TV commercial. Grace actually came up with it, not me."

At the mention of Grace's name, our smiles fade. Leo steps in and says, "All right, all right, you guys will have to agree to disagree. Let's go do some eating!"

David leads Leo toward a large buffet table and Connor trails behind. I hope he'll still be able to have a good time with Grace on his mind.

Rory runs over and grabs my arm. "Tell me everything!" she says, dragging me into the crowd. We weave our way through the dancers, balloons, and laughter floating around us. Six blown-up photos of David from when he was younger hang on the back wall. I stop to look at one of him with his father in a park somewhere warmer than here, judging by the palm trees in the distance. David looks about four or five. He's tossing a baseball to a tall, handsome man in a white baseball cap. They're both laughing. I glance at Rory. She's peering intently at something in the photo.

"What is it?" I ask.

She points to David's father's left hand, the one without the baseball mitt. "Look at his hand, how he's holding it really close to his body. He's in pain. His disease must have started to get worse around then."

I see what she means, but I never would have noticed it. That's one of Rory's special gifts. She sees things others miss. A few of Mrs. Goldberg's friends come over to admire the pictures and we step aside.

"C'mon," Rory says. "I want to hear what happened and we need to find Tara. She has big news."

Finding Tara should be easy. She's the tallest girl in the room, except for the grown-ups. Plus she's wearing my sister Kylie's dress. I spot her next to her cousin Emily.

Tara catches sight of us, too, and runs over. It's still weird seeing her in light blue. All she ever wears is black or brown with the occasional gray thrown in. "Guess what?" she says. Then without waiting for an answer, she shouts, "We're moving here! To Willow Falls!"

"What? That's great!" I join her as she jumps up and down. The stupid blackboard hits my chin but I don't care. Even though we've known Tara for only a few weeks, it was a pretty intense few weeks! I think we're the first group of friends she's ever had, and that makes it really special for all of us.

"My parents just told me after the service!" she says, beaming. "There's a house for sale right around the corner from my aunt and uncle's!"

"Which means right around the corner from David, too!" I tease.

"I guess it is," she says, as though she hadn't thought of that.

"Apple Grove looked amazing this morning," I tell her. "I bet he loved having his service there. It was a really great thing you did, putting that together."

"He seemed happy, right?"

Rory reaches out and squeezes Tara's hand. She blushes. I know how it feels when people ask me if I *like* Leo, or if I *like him, like him*, so I won't ask Tara if she and David are out of the friend zone. I'm pretty sure I already know the answer.

"C'mon," Rory says, "let's go down the hall to talk. I took a babysitting class last year in a room all the way in the back. I'll bet it's empty."

"One sec," I say, reaching into my bag for my phone. I text Leo, who is across the room stuffing his face at a buffet table.

OKAY TO TELL RORY AND TARA?

I watch as he shoves the rest of the food in his mouth and pulls out his phone. A second later he replies.

YES. STILL NOT DAVID, RIGHT?

I pause over the keys, then write:

I THINK WE'LL KNOW IF IT'S RIGHT TO TELL HIM.

I'm about to put the phone away when it dings again.

DAVID TOLD ME HE AND HIS MOM ARE GOING UPSTATE TO SEE HIS DAD TOMORROW. THEY'LL BE GONE A FEW DAYS, SO WE WON'T HAVE TO DEAL WITH IT.

PERFECT.

I put my phone away and convince them to wait a few more minutes while I get something to eat.

"Spill," Rory says when the three of us are finally hidden away in the back room.

So in between bites of French fries and hamburger sliders, I spill. I tell them what Angelina told us about failing to give Grace the benediction and about how she's in this frozen state. I tell them about the flash drive Leo "borrowed" and about how we need to go back to Grace's past birthday parties to fix what went wrong. Neither of them pushes me for the details of why we're able to do this. When it comes to our dealings with Angelina, we all respect one another's privacy. After the initial gasps of surprise at hearing that we're going back in time, that such a thing is even possible, Rory asks how they can help.

"I don't know," I reply honestly. "I have no idea what to expect."

"What happens if you run into yourselves?" Tara asks.

"We won't," I promise her. "We're only going to be at Grace's parties and I'm pretty sure I'd remember if I'd gone to one before."

Rory jumps up from her seat. "If you happen to wander off and run into me about a month before my twelfth birthday, please tell me not to mistake a drainpipe for a boulder at the Willow Falls Reservoir!"

I laugh. "Angelina gave us strict orders to get in, get out, and not make any changes. Plus, if you hadn't met Angelina that day, we wouldn't have gotten to be friends."

"Okay, good point," Rory admits. "Feel free to push me into the drainpipe if you see me, then."

"Poor Grace," Tara says, frowning. "Can we go visit her?"

"Her relatives are coming, so we might just be in the way." I'm about to suggest we get back to the party when all three of our phones ring at once. We reach for one another and grab hands. Our phones almost never ring since everyone texts instead of calls. All our phones ringing at once can mean only one thing.

A movie star has entered the building.

Chapter Four

"And David didn't mind Jake getting all the attention?" my mom asks as she runs the brush though my hair an
hour after the party ends.

"Nope. I think he was happy to turn over the spotlight."

Mom looks at me in the bathroom mirror as she evaluates
her work. It's been years since she's done my hair for me, but
when she offered to style it for the premiere, I said yes. Knowing
that I'll be telling her "almost truths" for the next ten days
makes me want to spend time with her while I can. Once the
"near lies" start, I'll want to keep my distance. That's just
the way it works.

"After the lunch part, Jake and Tara's cousin Emily performed their song from the play," I add, happy to have something
normal to talk about. Although for most people, being at the
same party with the cutest teen actor in America wouldn't be
considered normal. But for me it was the most normal part of
the day so far, which says a lot about my day!

"Sounds wonderful," Mom says as she smoothes some anti-
frizz cream onto the ends of my hair. "What else?"

"Well, then Jake convinced David and Connor to do their
number. They stuffed pillows from the community center's

couches under their shirts and ran around singing and kicking their legs out. David burst one of his buttons! It went bouncing across the dance floor." It was hilarious. And it was good to see Connor forget his troubles for a few minutes. "Then Bucky played the violin and Mrs. Grayson from next door played the piano. A bunch of the guys put David up in this chair, which is a tradition, I think. They even put his mom up in a chair!"

"Sounds like a great day," she says, laying down the brush on the counter. Then she says, "Wait, is Connor the older brother of the little red-haired girl, Grace? The one who played your youngest daughter last night?"

"Um, yes," I say, surprised. "Why?"

Mom turns me around to face her. "Honey, she's in the hospital. I don't know what's wrong, or how serious it is."

My jaw falls open.

"Don't worry, I'm sure it can't be too serious. This is Willow Falls, after all." She tries to smile brightly, but it quickly falls away.

"How . . . how did you find out about it?"

"This is a small town, hon. I knew before lunch."

The doorbell rings before I can find out what else she knows. "That's probably Leo and his parents." She kisses me on top of my head. "I'll offer his parents something to eat. You two can continue the game where you have conversations without actually speaking words to each other."

"You'll be happy to know that game is ending soon," I tell her, following her down the stairs.

"I'll believe it when I see it," she says. "Or rather, when I hear it."

Leo and I go straight out the back door while the grown-ups settle themselves in the living room. The last thing I hear before sliding the kitchen door shut is our dads making bets on whose kid will spend more time on the editing-room floor than in the movie.

We stop when we reach the middle of the yard. Neither of us has our blackboards on, which causes me a brief second of panic until I remind myself that we don't need them. Leo clears his throat. I clear mine. I suddenly feel really shy, which is crazy. He's been my best friend my whole life, if you don't count that one year.

He breaks the silence. "Hey, Amanda."

My stomach flips to hear his voice. Of course I've heard it all year, but not with my name included. I smile. "Hi, Leo."

"This feels . . . freaky. Good freaky," he clarifies.

"Yes, good freaky." I can't stop smiling.

"Crazy year, right?"

"And how about this going-back-in-time thing?"

He grins. "Totally insane."

"Are we really doing this?"

"I think we are."

We start talking over each other, saying anything that comes to mind just because we can. We don't even notice the back door opening until Tara and Rory appear. "Hey!" Rory shouts. "You guys are talking to each other!"

"Yup!" Leo says. "Just like regular folk."

"Don't worry," Tara says. "You guys will never be like regular folk."

I'm pretty sure she's right. "You know I'm always happy to see you," I say to them. "But, Rory, aren't you going to the premiere with Jake?"

Rory shakes her head. I can tell she put some extra effort into her hair. And she's wearing a really pretty sundress with strappy sandals. "He has to do press stuff before the movie starts. Like interviews and pictures. I don't want to be in the way."

"It must be bizarre having a famous boyfriend," Leo says.

"He's not my . . . oh, forget it."

We all laugh. "I promise I won't kiss my poster of him anymore," Tara tells Rory. "Now that you and I are friends." I can't help notice her slight hesitation before saying the word *friends*. She's so independent, much more than me. I think she's still getting used to having a group of friends now. I'm really glad she's staying in Willow Falls.

"I left your sister's dress in your kitchen," Tara tells me. "I hope she won't mind I wore it."

"She's away at a summer program for a few more days, so she won't even notice."

"She's not going to be at the movie tonight?"

I shake my head. "We're not really very close anyway."

"My mom and her sister have only seen each other twice in, like, thirteen years," Tara says, "but now they're, like, best friends. Maybe it will be that way with you guys when you get older."

"Maybe," I say. But I doubt it. I know Tara's trying to make me feel better but I've gotten used to it.

"Time to go, kids," Mom calls out to us from the kitchen window. "Pick a car and pile in."

We trudge inside, all talking together. "It's true!" my mother exclaims. She grabs Leo's mom by the arm. "Look! The kids are talking to each other again!"

"Let me see that," Mrs. Fitzpatrick says, pushing the husbands out of the way. "Okay, speak!"

Rolling his eyes, Leo turns to me, bows, and says, "Hello, Miss Ellerby. You look lovely this evening."

"As do you, Mr. Fitzpatrick." I give an awkward curtsy.

"No more chalk squeaking on blackboards!" Leo's dad says.

"No more texting at all hours of the day and night!" my mom adds.

Dad puts his hands together like he's praying. "Thank the gods above, it's over!"

Not the gods, I mentally correct him as we head out to the car. Angelina.

Chapter Five

The lights! The red carpet! The paparazzi's bulbs flashing in my eyes! Granted, no one actually wants to take *my* picture. The chances of me rising to fame are practically nil. I wouldn't want it anyway. I'd worry that every time I had a bad hair day (most days), I'd wind up on the front of some tabloid.

The red carpet extends from the center of the closed-off cobblestone street straight into the movie theatre's front door. The marquee screams PLAYING IT COOL STARRING JAKE HARRISON AND MADISON WATERS in foot-high letters. Usually our little theater gets only the movies that have already been out for months everywhere else. Getting one *before* it's even out, well, that's a Willow Falls first.

All thirty-five extras are supposed to go in together, so we're currently being held in this roped-off area to the left of the entrance. Our families and the other invited guests are gathered on the other side of the carpet. Tara and her cousin Emily wave from the front of the group. I feel bad that David's missing this, but Tara told us he went to the hospital to be with Connor before he and his mom leave town in the morning. I guess if anyone knows how horrible it is watching helplessly while a family member is in the hospital, it's David.

Next to me, Rory is squeezing her old friend Annabelle's arm with one hand and nervously twisting a pretty green earring with the other. A second later and she's on the ground, searching in vain for the earring that is now lost among too many feet. Annabelle and I share a smile. This is the Rory we know and love! I don't know Annabelle that well, but besides being super pretty and outgoing, she was a great friend to Rory last year when Rory was dealing with her own Angelina stuff. Stephanie was like that for me, during the year Leo and I were in a fight. I scan the crowd, but I don't see her. I'm hoping she's here.

"Here they come!" someone shouts. I think it was Rory's almost-five-year-old brother, Sawyer. He's sitting on his dad's shoulders, making him as tall as Tara's dad, who is the tallest man I've ever seen. Rory's and Tara's parents went to school together, with Leo's dad, too. I bet they never thought all these years later they'd be going to see their kids in a movie! Life is strange like that.

The limo pulls up to the front of the theatre and two official-looking men with headsets clear the path. One of the men opens the back door, then steps aside. At first all we see is a girl's leg, clad in a tall black boot. That's enough to get the crowd yelling and clapping, though. The leg turns into Madison Waters, the female star of the movie. She's a year older and may be even prettier than when she came here to film the movie. But I doubt she's much nicer. And someone should have told her it's weird to wear boots in July.

Jake climbs out next. He's changed out of the suit he wore to David's party and is wearing nice jeans and a black shirt that on anyone else I'd call a T-shirt, but somehow on him it looks dressy. He steps beside Madison and lifts his arm up to wave to the crowd. Everyone hoots and claps. He was popular before, but after helping the town raise all that money for our local community theatre by being in the play last night, well, he can do no wrong.

Madison scowls in obvious irritation at all the attention her costar is getting. She flashes a bright grin, slips her hand into Jake's, and plants a kiss right on his mouth! The photographers catch every move.

The cheers and shouts quiet for a second, before growing loud again. Now there are hoots, along with the shouts. Jake's cheeks redden, but he doesn't pull his hand away. Annabelle and I move closer to Rory, whose wide smile had only wobbled for a second. We each take one of her hands. She squeezes them gratefully. "I'm sure it's just for publicity," Annabelle assures her.

She nods, her smile still plastered on her face. A few more limos have pulled up and more actors from the movie pile out, along with the director who looks just as scary as I remember, the assistant director Brenda who I liked a lot, and a lot of other important-looking people in suits and dresses. They glance around them, probably wondering what the heck they're doing in our small town. A few of the women in heels twist their ankles on the cobblestones as they make their way toward the red carpet.

Jake and Madison start their walk toward the theatre entrance. Now that he's closer, I can see his smile has a definite element of a grimace to it and, whenever Madison steps too close, he steps away. It's a subtle movement, but I notice it. So does Madison, because her smile widens in an effort to counter it.

When the two of them are right in front of us, Jake stops and looks down. Then he pulls his hand free and bends over to pick something up. He opens his hand to reveal Rory's lost earring. "This is yours, I believe?" He stares Rory right in the eye.

She reaches out her hand for it, locking eyes with him. Madison looks from one to the other. "How did you know it was hers?"

He doesn't answer. Madison's eyes narrow as she looks at Rory. A few seconds later she says, "I remember you! You're that girl we were always laughing at! You kept falling down or swelling up. You were a disaster!"

Jake leans in closer and whispers, "But you're *my* disaster."

"C'mon!" Madison hisses, and yanks Jake away and toward the door.

"I can trip her if you like. I'm stealth, like a ninja." This is Kira talking, a fellow extra. She's been in Rory's debt ever since Rory suggested to the director that Kira looked enough like Madison from the back to stand in during a kissing scene.

Rory laughs. "I might take you up on that later."

·   ·   ·   ·   ·   ·   ·   ·   ·   ·   ·   ·

There's no more drama as we file into the area reserved for the cast and crew. As we take our seats, we're each handed a small bucket of popcorn and a reusable hard plastic water cup with a straw. Printed on the side of the cup is a copy of the movie poster.

"Hey, Rory," Leo says, leaning over me. "Your boyfriend's on my cup!" Everyone around us laughs. Some of the older kids, who were extras with us, look uncertain.

The whole room is buzzing with anticipation and it only grows as the theatre darkens and the movie comes on. The camera pans across the front of our school, though the sign over the clearly scrubbed and repainted entrance has been changed to THE RIDGEWOOD ACADEMY. I guess the Willow Falls school doesn't sound Hollywood enough.

I'm unable to eat any popcorn since I can't take my eyes off the screen for a second. Everywhere I look is something both familiar and "moviefied." Our school never looked so good. The colors are brighter, the halls wider. Familiar faces fill the corners of the screen while the action stays focused on the actors. Except when it comes to Rory! The camera lingers on her getting her leg bandaged on the soccer field. The scene where she gets hit in the face with a locker and Jake lectures her on the danger of texting while walking has the theatre howling with laughter.

Since they filmed the movie out of order, it was hard to figure out the plot while we were making it. Now I get it. It's your pretty typical teen romance: soccer star meets girl, girl wants to try out for boy's soccer team, boy feels threatened, girl dumps boy, boy realizes he's stupid, boy stands up to coach, girl gets on team, boy gets girl. It probably would have been just as good out of order! The rest of us extras can clearly be seen throughout the movie, often from the side or the back, but we know it's us. Usually we're doing something "studentish," like pulling books out of our lockers, or pretending to talk as we hurry to class. It's totally bizarre seeing myself on a huge screen, larger — much larger — than life. I try not to cringe at my hair, or whatever poor choice in outfits I happened to pick each day. I smile when I see my drumsticks tucked into my back pocket in a few scenes.

I make a mental note not to slouch so much.

In the dance scene at the end, the camera stays on our faces a little longer than usual. (Rory's in the far background in this scene because her ear was currently a few times larger than normal and she was hiding it under a jaunty little cap.)

At one point the boys (including Leo) are gathered by the dance floor. They are supposed to be gazing adoringly at Madison as she crosses the room. Leo, in a too-large suit he borrowed from his dad, is gazing right along with the rest of them. But when the camera pulls back, you can see the side of my face a few feet behind Madison. It's clear he's looking past her, right at me.

I hear a few giggles from the crowd, and someone whistles. Rory gives my arm a warm squeeze. I can't make myself look at Leo, so instead I look down at my lap and notice that my popcorn bucket is empty. I glance over in time to see Leo wiping his buttery fingers on his jeans.

"Thief," I whisper.

"Guilty as charged, ma'am."

The movie gets a standing ovation. The cast and a few people from the crew assemble up front where we're allowed to ask them questions. First the director thanks everyone for being so welcoming and accommodating during their visit. Then the mayor of Willow Falls goes up front and presents the director with a key to the city. It's a fake key, of course, but it's enough to make the director wipe away a few tears. A reporter from an entertainment magazine asks Madison, "Now that you and Jake are back together . . . will you be wearing your promise ring again?"

In response she flashes a big grin and holds up her ring finger. A large diamond glitters under the theatre lights. The crowd oohs and claps. Jake's lips form into a thin line. I lean over to Rory and say, "Not real. We saw her give him back the old one last year."

"I know," she whispers, still wearing her brave smile.

After a few more questions Jake says, "I'd just like to extend my personal thank-you to the Willow Falls community. I've gotten to know a lot of you during the time we shot the film, and since then as well. There's something special about this town and the people in it. I'm already looking forward to my next visit." He looks right at Rory when he says this.

Everyone claps wildly.

"Madison," the reporter shouts. "Will you be joining Jake when he comes back to town?"

Her smile falters for a second. "I'll have to check my schedule. I'm pretty busy."

All too soon one of the headphone guys ushers them out the back door and everyone stands up to go. Rory's brother is beside himself with glee, bouncing from foot to foot while people come up to Rory and ask if those injuries were real.

I bend down to pick up my pocketbook and manage to drop the contents all over the floor. My lip gloss, house key, phone, and Angelina's notebook skitter across the floor and under the row of seats in front of us.

"I'll get it," Leo says, already reaching for my phone. I examine it to make sure nothing broke while he gets the other stuff.

Rory elbows me. "I can get you a discount on a new one if you need it. I have friends in high places."

Rory usually breaks or loses her phone every few months. She's a legend at the phone store in town. "I'm good," I tell her as the screen lights up. "But thanks!"

She runs off to find Tara, and Leo and I meet our parents outside the theatre as we'd arranged. Mom gives me a big hug. "Let's go celebrate! Ice cream for everyone!"

I shake my head. "Leo and I have a summer job that starts tomorrow," I say, looking just to the left of my mom's eyes.

She looks surprised. "What kind of job? You didn't mention it before."

"We'll be helping out at little kids' birthday parties," Leo explains. "Like a bowling party one day, the beach the next, that sort of thing."

Leo's mom raises her eyebrow. "And they know you're only thirteen?"

Leo nods. "I think they wanted someone close enough to the kids' ages."

They nod, as though that makes some sort of sense. Now I can't meet *anyone's* eyes.

"Ray said he'd drive us each day," Leo continues.

"Who?" his mom asks.

"Roger St. Claire's assistant," my mom explains. "You know, the good-looking Australian?"

"Mom!"

"Oh, right!" Leo's mom says. "Now I know who you mean. He's a cutie!"

"What are we, chopped liver?" my dad asks, pointing at himself and then at Leo's father, who puffs out his chest.

"Remind me never to try chopped liver," Leo whispers.

"No problem."

"So where's tomorrow's party?" my mom asks.

"Bowling," I reply. "I think we need to be there by noon."

"Why don't we take you?" my dad says. "I haven't been bowling in ages."

"Let's double-date!" Leo's mom suggests.

Leo and I listen in horror as my dad brags about having his own bowling ball and Leo's dad brags about once having performed a gig at the bowling alley with his high school band that people in Willow Falls still talk about.

"Funny, I hadn't heard about it," my dad says.

"You must not travel in the right social circles," he replies, as though my dad travels in *any* social circles. They're having way too much fun ruining our plans.

Tara and Rory and their families join us. Rory's dad and Tara's dad are laughing and slapping each other on the back. Tara's dad makes fun of Rory's dad for having an orange stripe in his otherwise blond hair, and Rory's dad explains that it's some kind of bet gone wrong, but that it pays the cable bill. This explanation doesn't make any sense to me, but Tara's dad roars with laughter. I watch them and can't help thinking what it must be like to see an old friend after nearly half your life has passed. I can't imagine losing touch with my friends for that long. I look around again for Stephanie, but if she's here, I don't see her.

"Hey," Rory's dad calls to Leo's dad. "You remember Molly and Jimmy Brennan? They were a few years behind you in school."

"Of course!" Leo's dad says, pumping Tara's father's hand up and down and giving Tara's mother a hug. "Our bands played against each other in the battle of the bands one year!"

Tara's dad laughs. "You're right!"

"Welcome back to town!" Leo's dad says. "Come bowling with us tomorrow afternoon. We can catch up!"

"Sounds fun!" Mrs. Brennan says. "It will give me a chance to get to know Tara's new friends."

Tara grins weakly. "Um, I think Amanda and Leo have to work. Right? Maybe we should all go somewhere else?"

"Bowling sounds good to me," Rory's dad says.

"Bowling!" Sawyer shouts.

"But . . ." Leo begins.

"Don't worry, honey," his mother says, putting her arm around his shoulder. "We won't embarrass you two on your first day of work."

"We'll wait for the second day for that," my dad adds. "The beach, you said, right? My tan could use some work."

"Fab," I mutter under my breath. My phone dings with a text, so I turn away and pull it out of my bag. I can't imagine who it could be, since we're all standing right here.

HOPE YOUR ARM ISN'T TOO TIRED FROM SIGNING AUTOGRAPHS.

"It's from Kylie!" I say out loud, holding the phone out for everyone to see. I don't know who's more surprised, me or Mom.

Tara smiles. "Maybe you won't have to wait till you're grown up."

I text Kylie to thank her. As I slip my phone back into my bag, I get a nagging feeling that I'm missing something. While the parents coordinate plans for meeting tomorrow, I pull Leo aside. "Did you pick up the flash drive from the floor? It was in my pocketbook and now I don't see it."

He shakes his head. "I didn't see it on the floor."

"Leo and I have to run back inside," I tell our parents. "I left something at our seats."

I grab his arm and we go against the flow of people to get back in. We run down the aisle to where we were sitting and peer under each seat. The ushers are starting to sweep up, but it doesn't look like they've gotten to our section yet. I spot three quarters, a glove that must have been there since last winter, and a tube of lip gloss, but no flash drive. It would be awful if we came so close to being able to see what went on at the parties and then blew it.

"Found it!" Leo cries. He's on his knees two rows in front of where we'd been sitting. I run over in time to watch him pry it free from a wad of freshly chewed grape gum.

He reaches up to hand it to me but I back away. "No, thanks! Do you know how many germs are on that thing now?"

I can see the gears turning in his head. Does he try to chase me with it, like we were little kids and he had a spider? After what's clearly an internal struggle, he sighs and says, "All right, I'll get a napkin from the concession stand to wipe it off."

And my heart swells.

Chapter Six

The ride to the bowling alley is quiet. Or rather, the backseat is quiet. My parents are talking up a storm in the front. You'd think they never went out and had fun with their friends. And really, these aren't even their friends; they're an extension of *my* friends. Although now that I think of it, they rarely do go out unless it's family stuff. As I get older I'm starting to sense that being a grown-up isn't nearly as much fun as children want to believe.

Leo and I tried to figure out a way to convince them to stay home, but came up blank. The best we could come up with is to have Rory and Tara keep all the parents distracted so they don't notice that we're not actually in the building, even though we actually *are* in the building, just a year earlier. Sooo confusing.

Around six this morning it dawned on me that even though we know we weren't at Grace's parties in the past, we could still run into someone we know. Especially at some of the outdoor places, like the beach, where anyone could go. I texted Leo and we both ran around our houses trying to find whatever disguises we could. Sadly, all I came up with was a pair of plastic glasses with bushy eyebrows and a big nose attached that my dad used to wear when he wanted to make me and my sister laugh. I tucked it into my pocket just in case.

I'd downloaded all of the birthday videos last night and emailed the first one to everyone, including myself. I've been watching them on my phone with the volume off the whole ride. They are totally amazing. Mr. Kelly set up a video camera at every party! We can see exactly what went wrong each time. I don't know what we would have done without this. Oddly, most of the time it looks like Connor was directly involved. Like the one today, at the bowling alley, he walks away with the goody bags right before the end of the party and the kids leave empty-handed. Why would he do that? I wish we could just ask him without risking the collapse of the whole space-time continuum or whatever.

The others are already waiting outside the bowling alley when we arrive. The parents are comparing bowling balls and laughing about even *having* bowling balls while the kids huddle as far away as possible in the mostly empty parking lot. I don't see Rory even though her parents are here with Sawyer. We still have a few minutes before . . . well, before we do something I would have said is totally impossible. And maybe it is.

"Are you freaking out?" Tara whispers when I join the huddle.

Yes. But instead I say, "Nah. What's a little trip back in time?"

"Well, I'm freaking out for you," she says. "I'll do my best to keep the parents distracted so they don't try to find you."

"Knowing my mom," Leo says, "she'll try to get a picture of me working my first job."

The front door of the bowling alley opens and Rory runs out. "It's worse than we thought," she says breathlessly.

Our shoulders sag. "How could it be worse?" I ask.

"They don't have any kids' parties scheduled for today!"

We hadn't even thought about that.

"And almost all the lanes are open," she says. "Guess it's just too nice a summer day for people to think of bowling."

I glance at my watch hopelessly. "We only have two minutes left before the party starts and we disappear or something. You guys better get everyone inside."

Tara and Rory put on brave faces. "Good luck!" Tara says, hugging me. Her parents come up beside us. Her mother beams at me, which makes Tara blush. "You'll have to forgive my mom. She's never seen me hanging out with friends before."

"That's not true, honey," her mom says. "Well, it's been a long time, that's all."

"Have fun," my mom says, kissing me on the head.

"Try not to get fired in the first five minutes," Leo's dad tells him. "You tend to daydream."

"Thanks for the support, Dad," Leo grumbles.

"You all better get inside," I say hurriedly. "We're supposed to meet the party organizers out here and it would be really embarrassing to have all of you guys watching." I wince at having to tell them even a small lie like that.

Tara and Rory usher them inside and mouth, "Good luck," before the door closes behind them.

Leo and I hold up our synchronized watches. "Three ... two ... one," he says. I close my eyes. When I open them, I expect to find us in the same place, but with different cars around us.

Nope. Same place, same cars.

"Did we do something wrong?"

"Maybe we're supposed to go inside," Leo says.

"Okay."

He opens the door and reaches for my hand. But it happens too fast! He's gone! I stare at the empty space in front of me, then hurry through, heart pounding. What if Angelina's "tweaking" with our old curse didn't work right? What if we land somewhere else entirely? Or our atoms wind up in a billion different places, in a billion different times? What if we get stuck between here and there? Then and now?

A split second later I'm bumping into Leo's back. I look behind me through the glass portion of the front door. The window is streaked with rain. The mostly empty parking lot is suddenly full. My legs feel wobbly but otherwise I seem to be okay. Guess I shouldn't doubt Angelina's skills.

"Wow," Leo says, feeling his arms and legs, then touching my head and arm. "That really happened. And we're in one piece, so . . . bonus!"

All I can do is blink.

The bowling alley looks just like it always does. Twenty lanes, rows of balls on shelves, pinball and gum-ball machines, shoe rentals. It's crowded, though, and hard to hear very well over the constant balls rolling and pins falling. Still, I can hear Connor laughing. I follow the sound to the lanes farthest to the left, where I spot him helping a group of little girls lace up their bowling shoes. A big sign strung across the lanes reads, GRACE IS NINE!! WE'RE BOWLED OVER!! He looks a little shorter and a little thinner than our Connor. So weird.

"Well, here goes nothing," Leo says, starting to walk in the direction of the party.

I grab his arm. "We have to fix this thing with our parents first. If we mess up on the first day, they'll never let us out the rest of the week."

"But we tried for hours last night and couldn't think of anything."

I let out a long breath and look around. "I wish Rory had come back out with better news."

"Too bad it's such a nice day," Leo says. "In our present, I mean. It's raining here, and there's, like, one lane open. If our parents came today, they'd have had to go someplace else."

I grab his arm. "That's it! We can ensure they WILL have to leave. C'mon!" I pull him toward the front desk. The woman behind the desk is spraying something into a pair of bowling shoes. Without even looking up she says, "Shoe size?"

"We aren't here to bowl," I tell her. "We just need to book a party."

"We do?" Leo whispers.

The woman flips open a large notebook and picks up a well-chewed pencil. "When and for how many people?"

"A year from now. I mean today, a year from now. And the whole place."

She finally looks up. "All twenty lanes?"

I nod. "It's a big birthday party. We'll need the whole thing to ourselves."

"What time?" she says.

"Um . . ." We both glance at the clock. It's 12:06. If Angelina was right, and the past influences the future at the same time in both places, we'll need to build in a little time.

"How about twelve fifteen?" I suggest. "Till three."

The woman writes it down. "Last name?"

At the same time Leo and I reply, "D'Angelo."

She scribbles the info on a business card and hands it to me. "If you need to cancel, please do it at least twenty-four hours ahead."

"We won't need to," I promise. She's already back to spraying shoes. We hurry away.

"Brilliant!" Leo says.

"Do you think it will really appear in the book now? Like, in the future?"

"It's our best shot. Hopefully they'll see it and shoo everyone out, including our parents. C'mon, let's focus on what we came here to do." He strides off in the direction of the party.

"Wait, Connor is going to recognize us. I don't think my disguise is going to be very helpful." I pull out the glasses with the fake nose.

He laughs. "Let's save those for an emergency."

"What have *you* got?" I stare meaningfully at his empty pockets.

He scans the room. "Watch and be amazed." Reaching over to a shelf next to the counter, he grabs a Willow Falls Bowling Alley baseball cap and yanks it as far down as it will go, which basically just covers his eyes. "So? Can you tell it's me?"

"Seriously? Of course I can te —"

I stop talking because we're no longer alone. Connor has appeared right behind Leo. He taps his shoulder. "Hey, you work here?"

Leo, seeing my horrified expression turns slowly, keeping his eyes down. "Um, no?"

Okay, wow. We've been here ten minutes and have already broken Angelina's rule about talking to someone we know. Even though this time, last year, we didn't know Connor that well, we've still had classes together for years. He must not notice that we look a year older! But if he thinks Leo works here, this could be our chance to get closer to the party.

"Sorry to bother you," Connor says, and turns to find someone else.

"Connor, wait, he does work here," I say, stopping him. "We both do, actually. He was just kidding."

Connor looks down at his blue T-shirt. "How do you know my name? I'm not wearing a name tag, am I? Sometimes my sister likes to put a sticker with a name on my chest, and then people come up to me and are like, 'Oh, *hi, Hortense*,' or '*Hi, Octavio.*'"

"Um, no name tag. But we were in the same Spanish class all year."

He laughs. "Sorry, you must have me confused with the other red-haired kid in town. There were only fifteen people in Señorita Smith's class. I'm sure I would have noticed you."

Why is he acting like he doesn't know us? I turn to Leo to see if he's following this conversation, but he's not paying any attention. He's staring at his reflection in a glass case full of bowling trophies with a mirror in the back. Or rather, he's staring at the reflection of two strangers talking to Connor Kelly.

My jaw drops open. The jaw of the girl in the mirror drops open. I lift my hand to my mouth. So does she. I look at Leo, who totally looks like Leo, then I look at his reflection, and he looks completely different. The boy in the mirror has straight, shaggy hair instead of Leo's short curls. And he's wearing glasses and a preppy yellow shirt with a collar. I'm sure Leo doesn't own any yellow shirts. Or collars. I make a mental note to have a long talk with Angelina when we get back. She always leaves out the most important details.

"Are you all right?" Connor asks. "You look like you've seen a ghost. Or have my dashing good looks left you speechless?"

"It's the ghost," Leo assures him, slowly turning away from the mirror. "So what did you need help with? Ball stuck in the gutter?"

"We just need some help getting the kids' names up on the screen," Connor says. "Usually I'm good at that techie stuff, but I think it might be broken. Sure you guys are okay? You look kinda pale."

I can't seem to break away. The girl in the mirror doesn't look anything like me. She has curly hair, a pink flowery shirt, and are those . . . BRACES?? I force myself to turn away and answer Connor. "Sorry, I'm fine. We'll help you with the screen. I'm Aman . . . I mean *Amy*, and this is . . . Leon. It's our job to help at birthday parties."

"Great, thanks, c'mon."

"Amy and Leon?" Leo whispers to me as we follow Connor across the length of the room. "That's the best you could come up with?"

"Hey, you're much more likely to answer if someone calls you something close to your real name. Say, later Connor needs you and he'd be like, 'Hey, Doug, can I see ya for a sec?' And you're like, 'Who's Doug?' so you don't answer and you blow our cover because now he knows you told him a fake name."

He pats me on the shoulder. "That's my smart girl."

Miraculously, Leo/Leon manages to fix the screens. Mostly he gets lucky by pushing the right buttons in the right order. Mrs. Kelly asks if I wouldn't mind helping her set up the table where the girls are going to have lunch after they bowl. While I lay out the plates and cups, I watch her fill the goody bags with a mixture of candy and little toys like notebooks and glitter pens. Nothing looks enchanted to me, but Angelina works in mysterious ways. Clearly.

I pull Leo aside and point to the video camera. It's propped up next to the pile of gifts. It feels too risky to be so involved with the party when the incident with the goody bags won't happen for a long time. We slip away, unnoticed. Without discussing it, we return to the mirrored trophy case.

"You look cute in braces," Leo says, grinning at my reflection.

I run my tongue along my teeth. "It's so weird. I don't feel them at all."

He moves his finger on the bridge of his nose. In the mirror, his glasses rise up an inch. "Freaky. I don't feel these, either. It's like my hand is touching thin air."

"You look very smart with them on. Like a young professor."

"You're saying I don't look smart otherwise?"

"I'm just saying, you should get a pair for school. The teachers might give you better grades if they think you're suddenly smarter."

"I don't think it works that way."

Once we've stared at our strange selves for long enough, we move into the cafe area. After making sure none of the coins was minted after today's date, Leo treats us to an order of French fries. We find a table in the back where the sound of flying pins hitting wood is a bit muffled.

I munch on a fry and then ask, "Isn't time travel supposed to be, you know, more exciting than this?"

"You mean more exciting than eating soggy French fries in a noisy bowling alley that smells very strongly of dirty socks?"

"Yes, exactly. Like, aren't we supposed to be able to win the lottery now or something?"

He looks thoughtful. "We would have had to look up the winning numbers before we left, then when we got to the past, we would have had to buy the ticket. And, you know, be old enough to buy the ticket, which we're not."

"True. And I guess that would count as playing with the future, which Angelina warned us about." I pull another fry from the pile. "Well, there's got to be *something* cool we can do."

Leo shrugs. "After a year of not being able to do it, I'm just happy to be here talking with you. And by you, I mean Amy, of course."

"I wonder if Amy's getting French fries caught in her braces."

"Probably."

Chapter Seven

We finish eating and I duck out of the cafe to see what's happening with the party. "They're on to the pizza now," I report back. "A few more minutes to go."

"Should we just try to stop him now?" Leo asks. "I mean, why wait until he tries to steal them?"

"That's a good idea. Okay, you go distract him."

"Why me?"

"He sort of already knows you. I mean, he knows Leon."

"How am I supposed to distract him?"

"I don't know. Talk about whatever boys talk about."

"What is it you think boys talk about?"

"Sports? Girls? Sports?"

He rolls his eyes. "You forgot video games."

"Yes! Connor loves video games! Good, now go." I give him a little shove.

"Wow, Amy's bossy," he says, making a big show of stumbling forward.

The party area is bustling with activity. Girls are laughing and eating, Mr. Kelly pours lemonade, while Mrs. Kelly accepts a present from a tall but slightly stooped older man who must be Connor and Grace's grandfather. I remember him from the video, but the true brightness of his hair didn't come through on film. It's really weird seeing an old man with red hair, let alone fire-engine red hair. It doesn't exactly go with the wrinkles.

I search for Connor and find him on the floor, lining up the shoes to return. He really is such a helpful older brother. I find it hard to believe he would ruin Grace's birthday in any way. But videos don't lie. Leo/Leon sits on one of the hard plastic seats across from him and they start talking. I can't hear what they're saying, but Connor's not even glancing at the goody bags. I think this is going to work! One birthday fixed, only two more to go!

But then his grandfather goes over and tells Connor something, and he looks over at the goody bags and stands up. "No, no, no," I say out loud. But he walks right over to the goody bags and picks up the whole box. I watch helplessly as Connor carries the box away from the party and into a door marked OFFICE STAFF ONLY.

"Why didn't you stop him?" I ask Leo when he hurries back over to me.

"I couldn't. His grandfather told him to do it."

"What? His grandfather told him to steal the goody bags and ruin the party?"

He shakes his head. "No, of course not. Apparently the bowling alley gives each kid at the party a free pass to come back. The manager told his grandfather to bring the goody bags into the office so they can put the coupon, or whatever, into all the bags. Connor offered to carry the box. How could I have stopped him?"

"I guess you couldn't." We stand by helplessly as Connor comes back out of the room empty-handed. We watch the room for a few minutes, but no else goes in or out. "This is so weird. Why wouldn't Connor have gone back to get them, then? Maybe they got lost or something? Or given away to the wrong party?"

"Let's not wait to find out." He yanks me in the office with him. I expect to find someone stuffing the bags, but the small room is empty. No staff person stuffing goody bags, and worst of all, no box of goody bags at all! The box has vanished! Leo points to a back door marked EMERGENCY EXIT. "Maybe someone left through there?" He's about to push the door open.

"Wait, what if it sets off an alarm?"

"We'll have to take our chances." He gives the door a quick push and no alarms go off. The door opens on to the same view as the parking lot, just farther down. There's nowhere for anyone to hide. We peer into the drizzle. "I don't see anyone."

"Me, neither," I say. "On the video the next thing that happens is they realize the goody bags are gone and everyone looks around and then they kind of give up. Right?"

He nods. "Why wouldn't Connor just tell them where he brought them? It doesn't make sense."

We watch from a few lanes down as it all unfolds. They look around for the bags. They argue over who did what with them. It's not even worth telling them what happened, since we still don't know where the bags disappeared to. "So is that it?" I ask. "Did we fail our first time out?"

"Not necessarily," Leo says. "Angelina didn't say we had to replace the goody bags with the exact same goody bags, right?"

"No, I guess she didn't. But where would we get new goody bags? The kids' parents are going to be here in a few minutes to pick them up."

Leo looks around the crowded bowling alley for answers. "How much money do you have?"

I fish through my pockets and pull out two quarters and a dime. I hold them up. "What about you?"

"I have a dollar left after buying the fries. I didn't think about bringing money with us. We're going to have to do better with that next time."

We'll have to do better with a lot of things next time. "Well, what can we buy in a bowling alley with a dollar sixty?"

Leo points to the gum-ball machines a few feet away. "It's a tough call. You've got your standard rubber balls in multiple colors, your glitter stickers, or your temporary tattoos in the shape of beloved childhood television characters."

"They're SpongeBobs, aren't they?"

He nods.

"Let's go with the balls. They look like little bowling balls, to remember the party by."

"Sounds good," he says, feeding his dollar bill into the coin changer. "Even though they look nothing like bowling balls."

"Yeah, and you look nothing like you."

He looks up at me and grins. "You know what, Amy? You're right. I shouldn't have judged these little guys. Inside, we know we're Amanda and Leo, travelers through time and space, who —"

"Really just through time."

"Anyway! My point is, who's to say that inside these little guys there doesn't lurk a ball big enough to knock down ten pins at once?"

"Exactly!"

We feed the machine until we've got a pile of sixteen rubber balls threatening to bounce in every direction. The Kellys are still arguing over the missing — and presumed stolen — bags when we arrive. "Here," I say. "I know it's not much, but inside these little balls lurk the hearts of champions."

"They're like teeny tiny bowling balls!" Grace says, smiling up at me.

This is the first time I've really allowed myself to look at her since we've arrived. She doesn't look much different than she did when I saw her yesterday. Well, except for the whole catatonic state and all. She's been very brave about the fact that her goody bags were stolen. A lot of other kids would be having a tantrum.

I don't trust myself to say anything else to her, so I pile the balls into her hands, then scramble after the ones that roll off onto the floor. Connor bends down to help me.

"Thanks for your help," he says. "So you heard about the goody bags being stolen?"

I lean back on my heels. "Stolen?"

"Yeah, like from right in front of us."

"Crazy."

"I know."

He glances around to make sure no one can hear us. "Hey, you weren't really in my Spanish class, right?"

"Um, no, I guess not. I was confused before. Sorry."

"It's okay. It's just that, I'm sure I would have remembered you." It may be my imagination, but I think he's blushing.

"It's time to go," Leo says, pointing to the clock. "My shift is almost over."

I get to my feet. "Bye, Connor."

He waves and smiles at me a few seconds longer before turning away.

Leo leads me to the front door. "We only have a few minutes left to the official end of the party. That's when Angelina said we have to go back. If we miss our window of time, we could be stuck here. That would be a disaster."

"Uh-huh."

He waves his hand in front of my face. "Are you even listening to me?"

I grin. "I think Connor has a little crush on Amy."

He rolls his eyes. "Let's go, heartbreaker."

We swing open the door and together step outside into the bright sunlight. "Home!" he says, breathing deep.

Rory and Tara come running up to us.

"You did it!" Rory yells, jumping up and down. "We got up to the counter to get our shoes and they started making everyone leave for the private party! We all wound up at the diner, instead."

"How did you know we had anything to do with it?" I ask.

"The woman said the name on the party was D'Angelo!" Tara says. "We figured it out!"

"I feel a little bad about it now," I admit. "I mean, they must have lost a lot of money when no one showed up."

"We can have our birthday here next year," Leo says. "That'll make up for it. Sort of."

"How did it go in there?" Rory asks, tugging on my sleeve. "You went back in *time*! Was it totally amazing?"

Leo and I shrug. "Actually it wasn't all that exciting."

"Are you sure you did it right?" she asks. "I'm pretty sure it's supposed to be life changing."

"Really, the only strange part was that Connor didn't seem to remember he moved the goody bags right after he did it," Leo says. "He could have been lying, but it didn't seem like it."

"Also, we looked like ourselves to each other, but to other people we were like these totally different kids. Connor didn't recognize us!"

"Amanda had braces!"

"And Leo had glasses! And a limp!"

"I didn't have a limp!"

"You sort of did. Like a little shuffle."

He crosses his arms. "Harrumph."

"Don't worry, it was cute."

"I had a cute shuffle?"

"Okay," Rory says. "That's super weird. Tell us the rest while we walk back to the diner, okay? The parents made us promise we'd bring you right back after you got off work." She shudders. "You already missed two hours of listening to them reminisce about the good old days over chocolate chip pancakes and gravy fries."

"Bummer," I say, trying to look disappointed about that. Rory and Tara interrupt every few minutes but by the time we reach the diner, we've filled them in on what went down at the party.

"We need to go find Angelina," Leo says. "We have to find out if replacing the goody bags with the little bouncy balls worked."

"Okay," Tara says, "but don't have a yarn on the way. The oldies are getting restless."

Leo tilts his head at her. "Say what now?"

"Oops," Tara says. "That comes from living in a house with Ray for too long. Just hurry back."

She and Rory head into the diner, and Leo and I run across the street and down the blink-and-you-miss-it back alley. Angelina's shop is at the end. As usual it's filled with all sorts of merchandise, most of which has seen better days. Only people who have been involved with one of Angelina's "projects" can see inside the store window, though. To everyone else it's an empty building. That's another thing I'll have to ask Angelina to explain one day. But for now I'm willing to focus on the problem at hand.

The lights are off, but that's not unusual. "She could still be there," I say, reaching for the knob. Leo points at a small sign posted inside the window. GONE FISHING. BE BACK NEXT WEEK.

I lean my forehead against the cool glass and close my eyes. "She chooses *now* to go on vacation? How are we going to know if what we did today worked?"

"Actually, we already know," Leo says quietly.

I turn away from the window to find him holding up the little spiral notebook that Angelina gave us at the hospital yesterday. He has it open to the page with the bowling party. There is now a big red X covering the page from corner to corner. Scribbled on the side are the words, *Good try, though. Must do better tomorrow.* It's not even worth wondering how she was able to write in our book while we had it the whole time. If she can enchant goody bags, she can enchant a notebook. "Well, at least she's trying to be encouraging."

Leo takes my hand and tugs. "Let's go back to the diner. I think you could use some chocolate chip pancakes."

"*I* could use some chocolate chip pancakes?" I ask as we start walking.

"That's what I said."

I sigh. "I miss Leon."

He laughs. "You'll see him again soon enough."

"Make sure he wears his glasses." We both laugh, but then I stop right before we exit the alley. "What if we can't get her back? Grace, I mean."

"We will. We'll get better. This was only our first try."

I hope he's right. Tomorrow's party is at the beach. Angelina enchanted the balloons, and then the video showed Connor untying them and watching them fly away. Somehow we'll have to stop that. "You know what? I really *could* use some chocolate chip pancakes."

Leo squeezes my hand. "That's my girl."

He holds on tight the whole way down to the diner. This is the longest we've ever held hands. There are people all over the place, ducking in and out of stores, riding bikes or scooters, but all I can see are our hands. They loom as large as a highway billboard.

In unspoken agreement we let them drop before pushing open the door.

Chapter Eight

One place I didn't expect to find myself at 9 a.m. on Monday morning was the bottom of a huge hole. Yet that's where I am. Leo and I had come over to Tara's house early so we could plan for the party before Ray drives us to the beach. Tara ushered us right out here because apparently the house is crawling with grown-ups.

"Your parents seem really cool," I tell her. "I liked hearing about their adventures in Madagascar."

"I don't know about cool," she says, "but apparently when your parents leave you for a month to travel to the other side of the world, all they want to do when they get back is follow you around. They won't think to look down here."

"At least the rest of our parents came to their senses and remembered they actually have to work for a living," Leo says. "I couldn't handle a day of trying to dodge them at the beach."

We rewatch the video from Grace's beach party until Rory's face appears over the edge of the hole.

"There you guys are."

"Come on down," Leo says. "The water's fine."

Rory swings her legs over and then hesitates. "I'm really not the best climber."

Leo holds out his arms. "You can jump and I'll catch you."

"Um, I'll pass on that."

"David used to come down here to practice for his bar mitzvah," Tara calls up. "It's not as hard as it seems." She points out all the handholds and footholds we used and Rory slowly makes her way to us. She balances on one of the wooden planks that line the bottom of the pool and looks up at the clear sky. "It's pretty neat down here. Very private. Maybe I'll stay here instead of going to the beach."

"Really?" Leo says suspiciously. "You'd rather stay down here, where there are likely to be creepy-crawly things with many legs, instead of spending the day at the beach with us, your closest friends? There can only be one explanation for that."

At the same time the three of us yell, "Jake Harrison!"

"Yes?" a voice replies sheepishly.

We all whip our heads around and look up. There he is at the top of the pool, peering down.

Rory blushes. "Sorry, guys," she whispers. "He's leaving town tomorrow, so this is my last chance to see him."

"Does he want to come to the beach with us?" Tara asks.

Rory looks at me and Leo, a hopeful expression on her face. I know Tara did the polite thing by asking, but having a movie star with us would make it pretty hard to suddenly disappear. Or would it? I whisper so Jake won't hear. "That might not be such a bad idea. Everyone at the beach will be so busy watching him, they won't notice if two kids suddenly vanish."

"Unless they're taking a video of him," Tara says. "That's what I'd be doing." Then she turns to Rory and quickly adds, "I mean, you know, if I didn't know him as a person."

"We'd need to reveal him at just the right moment, though," Leo says. "Hey, Jake! Can you blend into a crowd?"

"Sure I can! I'll be right back." He starts to pull away.

"Give us ten minutes," Rory calls up.

He gives her a salute and disappears from view.

"Okay, quick," I say, "let's go over the plan before he gets back. I have twenty dollars in case we need money again. Leo, did you bring the duct tape?"

He unzips the backpack at his feet and pulls out a roll of thick gray tape. "Duct tape. Check!"

"Scissors?"

He replaces the tape and holds up scissors. "Check!"

"Handheld video game to keep Connor distracted?"

"Check and check." He holds up two different kinds.

"You guys think of everything," Tara says, impressed.

"We have to make up for yesterday," I say, taking out my phone. "Let's go over the video again to make sure we're not missing anything." I forward to the part where Connor unties the balloons from the back of the lawn chair. One minute he's helping his grandfather and parents set up some beach blankets a few feet away from the main party area. The next, he's marching straight up to the balloons. Unfortunately, he unties them before most of the guests even arrive. This leads to a lot of kids showing up late because their parents couldn't figure out where on the big beach to find the party.

"Hey, do you still have the video from the bowling party on there?" Rory asks. "Can I see it?"

I find the video and hand her my phone.

"So this is what a real phone feels like," she says, bouncing it gently in her hand. "Nice." She hits the PLAY arrow and watches for a minute while I help Leo repack his backpack.

"I was right!" she shouts, and holds up the phone. "Is this you?"

Sure enough, Amy and Leon are front and center in the video! Leo grabs the phone and gapes.

"I really DID have a limp!"

I grab it from him. "Wow, look how tall Amy is! I *thought* the ground seemed farther away!"

"I can't believe the video changed!" Tara says, leaning over Rory's shoulder. "That's amazing. And it's weird that we remember both ways. We do, right?"

We each take a minute to recall the memory of the first time we watched it. The rest of us nod. "Yup, it's still in my head, too," Tara says. "I wonder if the other people at the party remember both ways, or just the new one?"

Seeing the proof of our visit makes it all seem so much more real. When Leo and I were stuck in our eleventh birthday, anytime we tried to change the course of events, it didn't stick. Only on the last day were we able to make any real change, but that's because we were no longer stuck. Now we've actually changed the past for every kid at that party, even if only by the fact that they've had one more small rubber ball in their house for the past year.

Rory hands back the phone, frowning. "You are changing people's memories. That's so weird. It's like you're playing with their heads."

I'm not used to seeing that expression on Rory's face. It doesn't make me feel good. "But what choice do we have?" I ask. "If we need to change the past to save Grace, how can we do it without changing people's memories of events?"

"I guess you can't," Rory admits. "It's just . . . it makes me kind of mad at Angelina, playing with people's lives like this. I know that's dumb, I mean, she's just trying to help. I should be used to how she works by now."

"I know what you mean," Tara says. "You guys don't know the whole story with me and Angelina, and I'll tell you one day, I promise, it's just that, well, she controlled so much of my life without me realizing it. Like, my whole life she's been doing it."

We look at her, surprised. "Your whole life?" I ask. "But you've only been in Willow Falls for a month."

"My whole life," she repeats.

"Wow," we all mutter, then fall silent. I don't like being responsible for permanently changing someone else's life. What if one of those girls at the party stepped on her rubber ball in the middle of the night, slipped, and broke her leg? Or her dog chased the ball out an open front door and never came back? I suddenly feel really overwhelmed. My eyes fill with tears.

The girls rush over to hug me. "Did I make you feel bad?" Rory asks, stroking my hair. "I'm so sorry!"

"Was it something I said?" Tara asks. "Listen, the path that my family took to get to Willow Falls might not have been the one I'd have chosen. But it got me here, and now I have you guys for friends, and I think I even have a boyfriend! So Angelina can't be all bad, right?"

I squeeze Tara's hand, grateful for her words.

"I wouldn't be friends with you guys, either, if it wasn't for Angelina," Rory adds. "I know you and Leo were looking out for me last year. You even signed up to be extras in the movie so you could keep an eye on me."

I manage a smile. "You figured that out, huh?"

"Well, you kept popping up with random advice, and then I overheard you tell your friend Stephanie that you'd never seen a Jake Harrison movie before. That was a clue that you had other motives for being an extra."

"Uh, everything okay down there?" Jake's voice calls down. I look up, shading my eyes from the sun, which has moved overhead, but I don't see him yet.

"Dude, you gotta help me," Leo shouts. "They're getting all girly on me."

Jake appears at the edge of the pool. He spreads his arms. "What do you think?" It *sounds* like Jake, only this guy has shaggy blond hair coming out of a blue baseball cap instead of Jake's short brown hair. He could be Ray's younger brother. He's wearing dark sunglasses, an orange-and-red Hawaiian shirt, and the dorkiest pair of swim shorts I've ever seen on anyone over three years old. I mean, they have rainbow-colored rubber ducks on them.

"Now, *this* guy knows how to do disguises!" Leo says, tipping an imaginary hat at him.

"Impressive!" Tara says.

"He's had lots of practice trying to blend in," Rory explains. "He had that hat specially made."

"Is that real hair?" Tara asks.

"You'd rather not know," Jake says, grimacing.

"You might not want to smile at anyone at the beach," Rory suggests. "No one else has teeth as white as you."

He covers his mouth with his hand. "Ugh, my manager made me get them whitened. I'm getting them fixed as soon as the publicity tour is over."

Leo shakes his head. "The life of a movie star is never his own."

"Tell me about it," Jake says, pulling off the hat. "I'll meet you guys there. I have to do a phone interview on the drive."

He takes off and Ray appears. "Hey, you down there. Ready to stop playing silly buggers so we can get on the road? I have a committee meeting for the new community theatre when we get back and I don't want to be all beachy."

Leo scampers up the side and insists we were not playing silly buggers, whatever that is, but the girls hang back with me.

"Will you be okay?" Tara whispers. "I was going to say that you can always tell Angelina you're not doing this anymore, but I know from being in your shoes that you can't. You have to see it through and trust that Angelina knows what she's doing." She nods her head at Rory. "A wise girl told me that a few weeks ago when things were looking bleak."

"Thanks, guys," I whisper back. By the time I climb back out, I already feel better. I just need to keep my eye on the goal, which is fixing Grace. If I do that, I'll be okay.

When we climb out, Tara dusts herself off and asks Ray, "*You're* on a committee? No offense, but you don't usually work very hard."

"You're talking to the *head* of the committee," he says, sticking out his chest proudly. "I've changed my ways."

"Wow, direct one little play and suddenly you're Steven Spielberg."

"Who?" he jokes. At least, I *think* it's a joke. Hard to tell with him.

We pile into Ray's car and head out of town for the hour drive to the beach. We're halfway there when Tara gets a text from David. She reads it to us from the front seat. "Hi, Tara! Can you tell the others that Grace has been moved home? The doctors think she'll come out of it faster in the comfort of her own room. Since I'm up here with my dad, would you possibly be able to check on Connor and Grace for me? I'd really appreciate it. Have a great week and I can't wait . . ."

Tara's voice trails off. "Well, the rest is just for me."

Rory and I share a knowing smile. Leo rolls his eyes.

When she finishes reading, she says, "Well, at least now we have an excuse to hang around Grace."

I get a text from Connor right after, telling us the same thing about Grace being home, and also that she has an IV tube keeping her hydrated.

Leo leans over and asks, "Should we ask Connor if he remembers both versions of Grace's bowling party, like we do?"

I shake my head. "I don't think we should. It would really confuse him."

Ray says, "Still on that time travel thing? Boy, when you guys start a new game, you really commit to it."

Tara pats him on the shoulder. "You'll come around."

I text Connor to tell him that we'll come visit later and that we're glad Grace is home.

I had hoped that the beach would have been mostly empty. The less people, the less I need to worry about vanishing into thin air. Unfortunately it seems like half the state has decided today is the perfect beach day. Everywhere I look there are kids running, Frisbees and kites flying, sunbathers tanning. Jake's limo pulls up behind us. Not too conspicuous! Heads turn to watch.

Jake does a good job of sneaking out the door facing away from the beach, so by the time he joins us (in his disguise), no one is looking in our direction anymore.

Rory leans over and whispers something to Jake. He nods and says, "Hey, Ray, you can go whenever you want I can take everyone home in the limo."

Leo's eyes widen at the offer. "Sweet!"

Ray glances at his car and then the limo. He sighs. "Guess I can't compete with that. But no way I'm leaving before I get to see these two disappear into thin air!" He gestures to me and Leo and winks. Clearly he doesn't really believe us.

"What do you mean?" Jake asks.

"Leo has a fear of sand," Tara quickly explains. "So he always disappears with Amanda when they go to the beach."

I reach into my beach bag. "Luckily I always bring my sand-free beach towel, invented by none other than Tara's uncle!"

"Never met anyone afraid of sand," Jake says as we plunge into the sea of sunbathers.

"Couldn't you have picked something less embarrassing?" Leo hisses at Tara.

"I was going to tell him that you disappear so you can read your poetry to Amanda in private by the water's edge. Would that have been better?"

"You have a mean streak, Tara Brennan!" Leo says, his voice rising. "Writing poetry just proves I'm a sensitive guy."

"You write poetry?" Jake asks, overhearing.

"Not as much as I used to," Leo mumbles, reddening.

"I think it's cool," Jake says. "I've tried, but I'm not very good. Maybe you can teach me some tricks of the trade."

"Um, sure," Leo says. "We can do that when —"

"Hey, watch it!" a man's voice says as Leo's foot lands an inch from his belly.

Leo scrambles off the guy's beach blanket. "Sorry, sorry! I totally didn't see you."

I grab Leo's arm to steady him and fall right over an empty beach chair. "Oomph!" That kind of hurt. Leo reaches down to help me up.

"Um, Amanda? Where did our friends go?"

Chapter Nine

I spin around in a circle. No friends, and it's noticeably hotter. I didn't think our crossing into the past would happen so soon after our arrival. We had planned to have Rory distract Jake while we walked away. "Any chance you think Jake might not have noticed?"

"Probably not."

"Maybe he'll think we fell into quicksand," I suggest. "It could happen, you know."

"I don't envy Rory and Tara right now," he says. "But on the plus side, Ray must finally believe us."

We navigate around a clump of chairs and head for the party. The big helium balloons attached to a beach chair make it easy to spot. I recognize some of the girls, although they look a lot younger now that they are eight, instead of nine. Connor is about five inches shorter than he was at yesterday's party! He must have had a growth spurt during the previous year. I see their grandfather and mom, but I don't see Grace or their dad yet.

I spread out my towel a few feet away and we pretend to play cards. This would look more realistic if we actually *had* cards. "Do you have an ace?" I ask, then whisper, "How much longer, do you think?"

"Go fish," he replies, then under his breath adds, "We still have ten minutes."

So we watch out of the corners of our eyes, and wait. We don't want to risk interfering too much, so our plan is to get in and get out as quickly as possible. No chatting like last time. No giving gifts.

The sun is climbing higher, and the air is getting more muggy and sticky. I want to take my cover-up off, but I don't. Only a few months ago I wouldn't have even thought twice about sitting here in a bathing suit. Kylie was right when she told me once that being thirteen is complicated. I wonder for a second what everyone else sees when they look at me. Maybe Amy's wearing a bikini instead of my one-piece. But it's not like there are any mirrors out on the beach to tell me.

With five minutes left, we stroll over to the party. As practiced, I approach Mrs. Kelly and say, "Hi, I was sitting over there and noticed that your balloons look like they're coming off. I happen to have some tape, so if you'd like, we can tape them on and you won't have to worry." Leo holds up the tape and waggles it.

"Sure," she says. "That's very thoughtful of you."

Before she can change her mind, Leo starts wrapping the heavy tape around the base of the strings, securing them tightly into place on the back of the chair. Connor approaches and watches with interest. I inch closer, video games at the ready.

"Why are you doing that?" he asks.

"So they don't come untied and blow away."

"Oh." He keeps watching as Leo puts more and more tape around the corner of the chair. I tell Mrs. Kelly that we have scissors so she can cut it off when the party's over. Leo gives the balloons a firm tug to make sure they're secure before stepping back to admire his work.

Connor eyes the video games in my hand. "Want to borrow one?" I ask. He grabs them both but, instead of taking them away to play, he plops down right there, in the chair with the balloons on them.

Leo and I slowly back away. "Well, we didn't exactly get him away from the balloons," Leo says.

"True. But they're not going anywhere now."

"How much more time until he would have let them blow away?"

"About five minutes." We watch him carefully as more and more guests arrive. The party goes off without a hitch. Grace and her dad come out of the water and the relay races begin, which forces Connor to come out of his chair.

"One more minute," Leo says, noticing me squirming. I don't take my eyes off the balloons. The only people near them are a few grown-ups who I recognize from the last party, including their grandfather. He now has a beard and he looks as hot as I feel right now.

With only a few seconds to go, two little girls run up to the balloons and start batting them around. I stiffen. "Can they come off?"

"Not a chance. Someone would have to cut the strings with scissors."

I quickly rummage through my bag until I find the pair we brought with us. "Phew, they're still here."

"Three . . . two . . . one. We did it!" Leo yells in my ear. Then he holds up Angelina's notebook. I didn't know he'd brought it with him. "Look!"

I take the notebook from him. The page with the details about Grace's eighth birthday now has a big red check mark across it. "Yay!!" We jump up and down in the sand, not caring who notices. Some of the party guests glance our way but Mrs. Kelly is bringing out lemonade and that's much more exciting. As tempting as it is, I don't think we should ask for some. Leo has no such qualms and grabs two for us.

We drink them quickly and return to our hot towel. I fan myself with my hand, which of course does nothing. "Do you think it's okay to go for a swim?"

"We got our check mark," Leo says. "I don't think Angelina would care what we did as long as it doesn't affect anyone else." He pulls his T-shirt over his head and tosses it aside without a second thought. I wish it were that easy for me. I remind myself that this is Leo. We've been swimming together since our moms brought us to Mommy & Me class at the community pool in River Bend when we were fifteen months old. I pull off my cover-up and tuck it in my bag. "Race you," I call out, already running.

He catches up with me by the water's edge. Together we walk into the ocean. It's cold, but feels really good. I try to see my reflection, but the constant movement of the water makes it impossible.

"Hey, kid," the lifeguard calls out. It takes us a few seconds to realize he's talking to Leo. "You might want to take off your sunglasses before you go in any farther. If a wave comes and smacks you in the face, it could hurt. I've seen it happen. I'll hold 'em if you want."

"But I'm not wear . . . oh, right, got it. Thanks!"

Leo lifts up his (to us, invisible) sunglasses and hands them out to the lifeguard. To my shock, a pair of actual sunglasses appears in the lifeguard's hand. He tucks them in his bathing shorts and heads back to the lifeguard stand.

"That was crazy," Leo says.

"So crazy."

Leo grabs my hand. "Ready?"

I nod. We dive into the water. I stop caring about what I, or Amy, look like and just have fun with my best friend. We duck under waves and discover a sandbar to stand on where the water only comes to our waists. The only other people on it are a dad with his son riding piggyback. With his mass of black curls, the boy reminds me of a young Leo. The boy waves good-bye as they plunge back into the water. Over the noise of the waves and the people splashing in them, I cup my hands and say, "How weird is it that right now, back in Willow Falls, the current versions of ourselves are just going about their day?"

"I'll tell you one thing, they — I mean, we — aren't doing."

"What?"

"Talking to each other."

He's right! This is the Year of the Big Fight. It's mid-July now, so that's a little over a month since our birthday. I'm probably hiding down in my basement, banging my drums and feeling sorry for myself.

He steps closer to me, the water swishing around us. "I wish I could call myself up and tell myself to march over to your house right now and beg for your forgiveness. I hate that I hurt your feelings. You're the most important person in my life. I mean, you know, besides the people who gave me life in the first place. I was planning on writing you a poem about it — a better one than I wrote when we were eleven, but the summer has been so busy with Tara and everything that I never got the chance."

Leo's apologized before, of course, but never like this. I don't know what to say. A lone swimmer lands on our sandbar, then pushes right back off without giving us a second glance. "I forgave you a long time ago," I finally come out with. "You know that. We were just kids."

The water pushes us even closer together and I shiver, but not because I'm cold. My toes dig into the soft sand in an effort to steady myself. Leo's hand reaches out for my arm. Warm and strong, it keeps me from floating away. My eyes have to fight their way up his face until they meet his. How many times have I looked into those blue eyes? A thousand? A million? But it's felt different these past few weeks. Seeing Rory with Jake, and the way Tara and David look at each other when they don't think anyone's watching. And then the hand holding on the way to the diner yesterday. I know things are changing but I'm not sure I want them to.

A small wave pushes the water higher around us. Suddenly I realize that our math was wrong. We're back in time only two years. We would have to go back one more year to be in the midst of our fight. The versions of ourselves that we'd find today would have made up already. I should tell Leo, but I don't want to ruin this moment because it feels important.

My eyes still locked with his, I'm suddenly hyperaware of everything. The blue sky, the tiny bubbles on the water, my hair wet against my shoulders, the dimple on Leo's cheek that I'm so used to seeing I don't even notice it anymore. But I see it now. I see all of him. I shiver again.

"Are you cold?" Leo asks. "Do you want to get out?"

I shake my head slightly. "I'm fine. I just realized that we —"

And then his lips are on mine. The water and people and sky vanish. I'm not sure I remember how to breathe.

One kiss. And just like that, everything — and nothing — changes between us.

Chapter Ten

We return to our towels and wrap them around ourselves. My head is spinning. Leo kissed me. We *kissed*. I can't believe it actually happened. I keep stealing glances to see if I can tell what he's thinking. He looks completely at ease and happy. Not the slightest sign of head spinning. He spreads out his towel and we both plop down on it. I narrow my eyes at him. "You just kissed me."

He beams. "I know."

"You seem pretty pleased with yourself."

"Oh, I am," he says. "I've wanted to do that my whole life."

"You wanted to kiss me when we were four?"

"Yup."

"And when we were eight?"

"Uh-huh."

"But you figured you'd wait until we were thirteen, out in the middle of the ocean, stuck two years in the past with nothing better to do?"

"That's right. You got a problem with that?"

I shake my head. "But you know, I'm not sure it counts. We're not really us, here. I mean, basically Amy and Leon just had their first kiss."

He laughs. "We'll have to fix that." He leans across the towel like he's going to kiss me again.

I hold up my hand. "Still Amy!"

"Don't care," he says.

But before he reaches me, I hear two girls giggle. One says, "They're about to kiss!"

I assume they're girls from the birthday party, but then something about that voice makes me open my eyes. I didn't even realize I had closed them! The two girls giggling behind their hands aren't Grace's friends. I jump up from the towel so fast that I get dizzy.

"It's okay," Leo says, pulling me back down. "They won't recognize us."

"C'mon, Stephanie," the shorter girl in the red two-piece says, "let's go practice."

Apparently no longer interested in us, the two girls walk to an empty patch of beach a few feet away and start doing cart-wheels. A part of me wants to go running in the opposite direction, while another part wants to run up to Stephanie, pull her away from Ruby — who has still never really been nice to me — and tell her all about what happened on the sand dune. Next to Leo, she's been my best friend my whole life. This past year was the first time we didn't sit together at lunch. I miss her.

"Are you okay?" Leo asks.

I can't help staring at them. I just saw Stephanie a few days ago when we did the play together. This version of her looks like a kid, not a teenager. Two years ago, they'd have just made the gymnastics team. Stephanie was so excited about it. Ruby moves on to back handsprings. She always was amazing at those. "Keep your hands straighter!" a woman yells from a beach chair nearby. Judging by their matching black ponytails, I'm going to guess that's her mother.

Ruby tries again. It looks perfect to me.

"You can do better than that," the woman scoffs. "You want to get cut from the team already?"

Stephanie backs away, looking uncomfortable. "Um, I'll be right back," she says. Ruby barely notices. She's too busy trying to please her mother. I actually feel a little sorry for her. Stephanie always said Ruby wasn't as bad as I made her out to be. Maybe she feels sorry for her, too.

I watch Stephanie dig into her beach bag and come up with her phone. I remember she got hers a few months before I did. She turns her back to Ruby and punches in a number.

"Hi, Mrs. Ellerby," she says. "Is Amanda there?"

"It's almost time to go," Leo says, but I can't turn away.

"She's calling *me*!" I whisper.

"I know, but maybe it's not right to listen."

Connor suddenly appears at our towel. Leo and I both whip our heads toward the party. Thankfully the balloons are still there.

"My sister's party is almost over," Connor says. "My mom told me you have scissors? Can you cut the balloons off so I can fold up the chair?"

"Sure," Leo/Leon says. "I'll bring them right over."

Connor nods and runs back to his family. While Leo digs through his beach bag, I inch closer to Stephanie.

"Okay," she says to my mom. "Just tell her I called." She tosses her phone back in her bag. Ruby sidles up to her. "She's hanging out with Leo again, right?"

Stephanie nods.

"I'm not really sure why you stay friends with her."

My heart sinks. I'm the worst friend. Stephanie has a right to hate me.

"Amanda's great," Stephanie says. "She had a really hard time last year after Leo said those things. I can't blame her for wanting to make up for lost time. She was there for me when my parents weren't getting along and things were really weird at my house. We'll always be friends, even if it won't be the same."

Ruby shrugs. "Whatever. Let's keep working on your front handspring. Your feet aren't lined up right."

My heart swells. I don't even blame her anymore for not coming to the premiere Saturday night.

Leo tugs at my arm and I finally turn away from eleven-year-old Stephanie for good, with a plan to be a better friend to the thirteen-year-old one. I pack up our bags while he collects the video games from Connor and cuts the balloons off the chair. I see him hand all but one of them to Grace to take home with her. He returns with a handful of wadded-up tape and a single red balloon. "For you, madam."

"The tape or the balloon?"

"Your choice."

I reach for the balloon.

"A wise decision."

We swing our bags over our shoulders and head to the spot where we'd first appeared two hours ago. The same guy is still there, but at least this time he's lying on his belly. If anything, the beach is more crowded now, though. I have no idea how we'll just suddenly disappear and expect no one to notice.

"I got this," Leo whispers. He cups his hands together and shouts, "Hey, is that Jake Harrison?" He points in the opposite direction, jumping up and down for emphasis. Two years ago Jake had just starred in his first movie and already everyone knew him. Well, everyone between ten and fourteen. At once, all the girls in earshot start running, which means their parents have to run after them.

"Nice work."

"Thanks," he says. "And it's not even a lie, because right this minute Jake Harrison really IS at the beach! Only two years in the future."

"C'mon, let's go meet that future." Now that no one is even glancing in our direction, Leo and I turn around, take two steps, and land facedown, our mouths full of sand.

Chapter Eleven

Our limbs are tangled, my face is in the sand, and my balloon is underneath me, squashed flat as a pancake. I try to open my eyes but sand starts to leak in, so I quickly close them again. We must have done something wrong. Gone in the wrong direction, then tripped and fallen. "Did we miss our chance to get back?" I ask Leo, spitting out sand with each word. I can feel the panic rising in my chest.

"We must have," he says, his head somewhere close. "I think we might seriously be stuck here!"

My heart starts pounding. Stuck in the past! "What do we do? Should we go home and try to explain to our parents why there are two of each of us?"

"We can't," he says, his voice tight, like he's holding in tears. "They'll just see Amy and Leon. They'll think we're crazy."

"Oh, no, you're right!"

His hand finds mine. "Don't worry, Amanda. We'll get through this together."

I squeeze his hand and feel better, like always. I'm scared, but I'm not alone. "We'll find Angelina. She'll know what to do."

We lie still, not ready to face what's ahead.

"Okay, you guys are being seriously dramatic," says a voice from above.

I twist my head to the side and try to open my eyes again. All I see is a blurry face with brown hair, far away in the distance. "Rory? Is that you?" I rub at my eyes.

"I'm here, too," Tara calls out.

Relief pours through me. "What happened?" I shout. "Where are we?"

"You're in a hole!" Rory says. "We spent the last two hours digging it."

Leo starts to laugh, then coughs as he chokes on more sand.

"It was my idea," Ray says. "We did it so no one would see you appear again. Totally brill, if you ask me."

"Ray has adjusted to all this very well," Tara says. "All he did was shout, '*holy dooly*,' when you disappeared, but that was it. Here, I'm lowering down a wet towel for your eyes."

Leo helps me sit up and we both grab for the towel. Once my eyes are relatively free of sand, I survey our surroundings. We are indeed in a deep hole. Not pool hole deep, but it's definitely not your average hole in the sand at the beach.

I feel a little silly for overreacting. Some advance notice might have been nice! Not that I can imagine how they could have warned us, but still.

Ray leans over and helps Leo up, then both of them help me climb out. I'm disoriented when I reach the top. The air is much cooler in the present. And no one is running in search of a movie star. Speaking of movie stars . . .

"Where's Jake?" Leo asks, taking the words out of my mouth.

Rory points to a beach chair with an umbrella attached to the back. Leo and I walk to the front of it.

"How ya doing, Jake?" Leo asks.

Jake, still in disguise, stares straight ahead and grunts. The others join us.

"He's away with the pixies, I'm afraid," Ray says.

I look to Tara for a translation. "He's in some other world," she explains. "He's been like this since you guys disappeared into thin air."

Rory snaps her fingers in front of his face, then pats his arm. He doesn't give any indication that he's aware of anything around him.

I turn to Leo. "He looks like Grace did. I mean, not his expression. But if seeing us made him freeze up like this, maybe Grace saw something, too."

"We were all at the bar mitzvah together, though," Tara points out. "If Grace saw something that freaked her out, wouldn't we all have seen it?"

"I guess. Well, what are we going to do about Jake? We can't leave him this way."

"I know what we do in Australia when someone zones out like this," Ray says. He lifts Jake's hat off his head and pours an entire bottle of water on him. Then he pushes the hat back on and stands back.

Jake springs to life, sputtering and wiping water from his eyes. "Really, dude? You could have just nudged me awake." Jake pulls his sunglasses from his shirt pocket and slips them back on.

"You did it!" Rory shouts. Then she runs and throws her arms around Jake.

"Wow, if I knew I'd get a greeting like that, I would have taken a nap in the sun a long time ago." He looks over Rory's head at us. "Hey, you guys are back. That was a long walk."

We all exchange uneasy glances. Is it really possible his brain has made up an excuse for our disappearance? "Um, yeah, long walk," Leo agrees. "Took a swim. Had some lemonade."

Jake's cell phone rings. He steps away to answer it and nearly trips over the huge mound of sand that came out of the hole. He gives a little yelp as he catches his balance and then calls out, "Hey, you can't have a hole like that with Rory around. That's just asking for trouble."

Rory sighs happily. "My hero. Always looking out for me."

"Nah," Tara says. "He just doesn't want you to steal all the scenes in his next movie, too."

"I don't think he has to worry. Although I do still have that eye patch. Sawyer uses it when he plays pirate."

"So he really thinks we went on a walk?" I ask, glancing over my shoulder at him. He seems to be having a very animated phone conversation. "And that he was asleep for two hours?"

"It sounds like it," Rory says. "I think I'd know if he was making it up."

"But, Ray, you saw everything, right?"

Ray nods. "One minute you guys were there, then, poof, gone."

"And it didn't freak you out?" I ask.

"Well, you guys had warned me. I just didn't believe you. I believe you now, by the way."

"Gee, thanks," Leo says.

"Anytime, mate."

"Thanks for sticking around, Ray," Tara says.

"Couldn't leave ya with Jake in that condition." He flexes his arms. "Plus you needed my brute strength to dig that hole."

"We should fill that back in." Leo reaches for the plastic shovels they must have borrowed to dig with.

Jake rejoins us. "Rory, can I talk to you for a sec?"

The two of them walk to the other side of the umbrella. The rest of us hurry to fill the hole back in while trying not to eavesdrop. Eventually we give up on the shovels and just push huge mounds in with our bodies. I am literally covered head to toe in sand now. The things I do for Angelina! I'm still confused, though. "If Ray saw us and he's fine," I whisper, "why did it make Jake go into shock like that?"

"I've been thinking about that," Tara says. "I think some people just aren't allowed to see anything that has to do with Angelina. Like David can't see all the stuff inside her store, or smell the apples at Apple Grove. But Angelina gave Ray that money to drive us, so maybe that was her way of allowing him in."

Ray sniffs the air. "I don't smell any apples. Just suntan lotion and wet sand."

Jake and Rory return. She looks sad but explains that Jake has to go straight from here to the airport.

"No ride in the limo?" Leo asks, pouting.

"Sorry, guys. Next time, okay?"

The guys load up the chairs and towels, and then Jake returns the shovels to a family of four girls sitting a few blankets away. They have no idea that they just spoke with Jake Harrison the movie star.

The rest of us say good-bye to Jake, then pile into Ray's car. We leave the front seat open for Rory, who is still saying her own good-bye. I lean forward. "Ray, can you take us to Grace's on the way home? We can bring some food or something."

Tara shakes her head. "I texted Connor while you were gone. He said that Grace seems peaceful, but it would be better if we came tomorrow, instead. They're still getting her settled at home."

"Oh. Okay." I'm always relieved when, even if the report isn't much better, it's not any worse.

When Rory comes back in, no one even teases her because she looks so bummed. "When will you see him again?" I ask.

She brightens a little. "Tonight, actually. We're going to video chat when his plane lands."

"Why did he have to leave so suddenly?" Tara asks. I'm glad she asked because I wanted to know but didn't want to seem nosy.

She frowns. "It's Madison. She's making him go to this event tomorrow for the movie. She was supposed to go alone but now she said it wouldn't look good if her 'boyfriend' wasn't there."

"I know what will make you feel better," Leo says. He whips out Angelina's notebook and shows her the page with the check mark on it. "We did it this time! And we managed not to change anything else in the process!"

She smiles. "I'm glad."

I elbow him. "That's not going to help her feel better."

"You can't blame a guy for trying!"

"I know," Tara says, "we'll hang out tonight, and we'll do something really girly, like paint our nails all different colors or straighten our hair. We'll invite Annabelle and Sari. You know, your normal friends? They can bring all their makeup and hair stuff. It'll be fun."

Even though she doesn't have much experience with having friends, Tara is a fast learner. She's totally not the nail-painting, hair-straightening, hang-with-a-group-of-girls-she-doesn't-know type, but she knows what would keep Rory distracted.

"So I take it we're the 'not normal' friends?" Leo asks.

"Definitely," Tara says.

He nods. "Yeah, I can see that."

"Are you in, Amanda?" she asks.

"I can't. Kylie is coming home from her summer program. We're going out to dinner."

"I feel left out of this plan," Ray says, glancing in the rear-view mirror at Leo. "How 'bout you?"

Leo holds up his sand-filled fingernails and pretends to admire them. "I don't need to go. My nails are already perfect."

Rory laughs, which I take as a good sign that we're cheering her up.

"So what did you do at the party after taping the balloons?" Tara asks. "You still had a lot of time left, right?"

Leo and I avoid each other's eyes. "Um, we didn't do much, really," he says. "Played cards, swam in the ocean, the usual beach stuff."

"It was really hot there," I add. I want to tell them (well, not Ray!) about what happened on the sandbar, but I want to keep it to myself a little longer. Luckily Tara asks Ray to tell us about his job as the head of the new Willow Falls Community Theatre and I can lean back and just think. I'm very aware of Leo breathing next to me. I feel the corners of my mouth turn up. Without looking, I can feel him smiling, too.

* * * * * * * * * * *

Dinner with my parents and Kylie goes on much longer than I'd like it to. Normally I love going out to dinner since we don't do it very often, but I really want to get home and call Stephanie. After seeing the eleven-year-old version of her today, I'm really missing her. Kylie spends the first half hour talking about what she learned at her two-week-long performing arts camp. Then I have to spend the next half hour telling her about the play on Friday and the bar mitzvah and the premiere.

"Wow," she says. "I missed a lot in a week! I promise I'll be the first to buy a ticket when the movie opens next month."

"Look at our girls," Mom says, beaming at us across the table. "Getting along so well, talking like friends."

Kylie and I force smiles. We both know it won't last long.

It lasts, in fact, just until we get back home.

"Why is my blue dress in a heap on the floor of my room?" she asks.

Oops! I had meant to hang it back up before she noticed I took it.

"And it has a stain right here." She holds up the sleeve. "Did you wear this?"

"No," I reply honestly. "But my friend Tara didn't have anything to wear to the bar mitzvah and I didn't think you'd mind."

Okay, I knew she'd mind. "I couldn't let Tara go in shorts and a T-shirt, which was pretty much all she had."

Kylie sighs. "Fine, whatever. Owen says I get angry too easily. I'm trying to work on that."

I don't know who this Owen is, but I like him already. "What happened to that guy Will? Wasn't he your boyfriend when you left for camp?"

She shakes her head and tosses the dress into her hamper. "Will was, like, two months ago. And Brett was the one right before Owen."

"So you broke up with Brett for Owen?"

She flips open her suitcase and nods. "I felt bad about it at first, but Owen and I are, like, soul mates."

"Soul mates? How do you know?"

She shrugs. "When you know, you know."

"Oh." I turn to go.

"Amanda," she says, "I know it's not my business, but I think Leo is holding you back."

I slowly turn around. "What do you mean?"

"Having a boy as a best friend is going to keep other boys from asking you out."

I have no idea what to say to that. Kylie's never talked to me about boys. Ever.

"Um, okay. I'll keep that in mind."

"It's just that you're thirteen now, and you've never even mentioned liking anyone. I had my first boyfriend when I was your age. Remember? That kid Jonathan?"

I nod. I definitely remember Jonathan. "Why did you stop going out with him? He was nice."

"Oh, Amanda," she says, shaking her head. "No one stays with their first boyfriend!"

I *really* don't want to have this conversation. "I'm sorry I borrowed your dress," I say instead. "Tara really appreciated it, though."

She shrugs. "Just ask next time."

"Okay," I say, and hurry to my room. I see the journal Kylie gave me a few years ago sitting, still unused, on my dresser. I wonder if I'd taken her advice and used it, it would be easier to sort out my feelings. I close my door and fish my phone out of my pocket. I might not be able to sort out the Leo thing yet, but I can sort out something at least.

"I'm really, really sorry," I tell Stephanie as soon as she picks up.

"No, *I'm* really sorry," she says. "I should've come see you after the movie. I was in the back with Mina and Ruby, and they wanted to go to the diner right after to meet the other girls from the team. But you were great. I mean, it was really fun seeing you up there on, like, a ten-foot-tall screen. Why are *you* sorry?"

"For not being a better friend. For ditching you when Leo and I made up."

She laughs. "That was over two years ago. And you didn't ditch me. I got busy with other stuff, too. And whenever we do get to hang out, it's like no time has passed."

"Thank you for saying that."

"Hey, you're stuck with me. No one knows me like you do."

"Same here," I say, my throat tightening. "Thank you for doing the play on Friday. You were great."

She laughs again. "I totally blew my lines and started doing last year's tumbling routine onstage! I'm pretty sure there are no cartwheels in *Fiddler on the Roof.*"

"There are now!"

"Hey, how was David's bar mitzvah?" she asks.

"He did great, but there's something else I want to tell you about first." I take a deep breath. "Leo kissed me."

"What?" she shouts into the phone. "Holy smokes! Finally!!"

I smile, glad I decided to tell her.

"Well? How was it? I'm dying here!"

"It was . . . salty."

"Salty?!"

So I tell her the story of our ocean kiss. We never do get around to talking about the bar mitzvah.

Chapter Twelve

I wake up to a text from Leo. We'd emailed last night to go over the plan for today's party at Mr. McAllister's Magic Castle Birthday Party Palace, so I didn't expect to hear from him this early.

I JUST WANTED TO SAY THAT YESTERDAY WAS PERFECT. THANK YOU.

I smile and bring the phone back to bed.

YOU MEAN THE PART WHERE WE KEPT THE BALLOONS FROM BEING UNTIED?

LOL. NO, NOT THAT PART.

SWIMMING IN THE OCEAN? IT REALLY WAS REFRESHING. HOT DAY.

YES, THE OCEAN. I AM THANKING YOU FOR THE OCEAN.

YOU'RE VERY WELCOME.

FINE, I GET IT. YOU DON'T WANT TO TALK ABOUT IT. WHAT TIME ARE WE MEETING RORY AND TARA AT THE DINER?

11.

I'LL COME OVER AND WE CAN RIDE TOGETHER.

OK.

I'm about to set down the phone when another text comes in.

HEY . . . DID YOU TELL ANYONE? YOU KNOW, ABOUT THE REFRESHING WATER?

I hesitate before writing back.

STEPHANIE.

He doesn't reply right away and I start to worry that maybe he didn't want me to tell anyone. Finally my phone dings.

I TOLD SOMEONE, TOO.

WHO?

MY MOM. I COULDN'T HELP IT! SHE KNEW SOMETHING WAS UP THE SECOND I WALKED IN.

I groan and lean back on the pillow. I'm never going to be able to look Mrs. Fitzpatrick in the eye again. When Leo arrives on his bike, I don't even let him get close to the house in case he decides he can't keep secrets from *my* parents! I grab my backpack and meet him on the driveway. "We have one job today," I say, slipping on my helmet. "Keep Connor occupied while the magician pulls the rabbit from his hat and we're golden." I can't imagine why Angelina decided to enchant the magician's bunny or why our video showed Connor leaving with it, but we'll soon find out.

"I'm kind of looking forward to going back to Mr. McAllister's," Leo says, riding in circles around me while I strap my backpack to my bike. "Do you think he'll remember us?"

I laugh. "From when we turned one? He must have had a thousand birthday parties there since ours."

"Yeah, but I bet we were the cutest birthday kids."

"We were pretty cute," I admit, thinking of the picture in my album of the two of us taking our first steps together. All these years later, we're still taking first steps together. I wonder if Mr. McAllister would have foreseen *that.*

When we arrive at the diner, Tara and Rory are pacing outside. Leo and I pull off our helmets and lean the bikes against the window. "What's wrong? Is it closed?" I've never seen the diner closed in my whole life.

They shake their heads. "You'll never guess what's inside."

"What?" I ask.

They swing open the doors and push us into the small waiting area. Everything looks the same to me. And then I spot it. "No!"

"Yes!" Tara says, lifting the cane with the handle shaped like a duck's bill out of the umbrella stand. "It's back!"

"How? You returned it to Angelina after the play, right?"

"Yes!"

"And it wasn't here on Sunday, right? When we came with our families?"

"It definitely wasn't," Rory says. "You know how Sawyer always used to quack when he saw it? Well, he noticed right away that it was missing and I had to tell him it had been returned to the woman who owned it."

"But Angelina's out of town," Leo argues. "She couldn't have left it here again."

The door to the kitchen swings open and Annie, the diner owner's daughter, comes out. She grabs four menus. "You guys ready to try something other than chocolate chip pancakes this time? Something healthier for growing bones?"

Tara rushes up to her with the cane in her hand. "Annie, remember last month when you gave me this cane in exchange for us helping your daughter sell all those cookies?"

Annie looks at Tara like she's suddenly sprouted six more heads. Then she looks at us. "Is your friend okay?"

"You really don't remember?" Leo asks. "We dressed up in those Sunshine Kids uniforms that totally didn't fit any of us? I still have nightmares about it."

Annie shakes her head slowly. "That cane's been here since before I was born."

"But . . . I . . . we . . . it . . ." Tara stumbles over her words. I gently reach for the cane and slip it back in the umbrella stand.

"Sorry, Annie," I tell her. "We were just confused. We'll see you later."

"We only have a half hour to get to the party," Leo says as the four of stumble back out to the sidewalk. "We'll have to figure this all out later."

"There's only one explanation I can see," Rory says. "Angelina must have gone back in time herself."

"But if she could do that," I ask, "why is she sending us?"

Rory shakes her head. "As usual, Angelina only tells us half the story."

"Not even!" Tara scoffs.

"Why don't you guys go try to find her," I suggest. "Check the store, the historical society, all her usual haunts. Leo and I can handle this one alone."

"What do you have to do at today's party?" Rory asks. We hadn't gotten a chance to show them the video yet.

"You'd love it," Leo says. "We have to make sure Connor doesn't steal the rabbit from the magician's hat!"

Rory shudders. After an incident with a pet rabbit, she is no longer a fan of bunnies. "You're on your own, then. Good luck!" She drags Tara away from the diner window, where she's staring at the cane. "C'mon, you're starting to make the customers nervous."

Mr. McAllister's Magic Castle Birthday Party Palace is a very popular place in town for parties. It's only closed on Tuesdays, which means that whatever day of the week it was for Grace's seventh birthday, it wasn't a Tuesday. Leo tries the front door. It's locked. We sit on our bikes and wait.

"Let's go over the plan," I suggest. For some reason I feel the need to keep talking. I think I'm afraid of it being awkward otherwise.

"We don't have time," he says. "It's starting. Look."

I look up and almost fall off the bike. The empty parking lot is suddenly full of cars. The sound of kids laughing and running around reaches us from inside. "Well, let's go. We've got a rabbit to protect."

Leo chuckles and says, "Hey, we just brought our bikes back in time three years."

I look down. "You're right! I hadn't even thought of that!" We lock them up to a skinny tree and push through the door. Inside, kids are running everywhere. It looks like there are two parties going on at once. A whole group of toddlers is playing on the inflatable slides and the castle-shaped bouncy house, while Grace's guests are gathered on the other side, dancing around and waiting for the magician to start.

"We have to blend in," Leo whispers. "Hopefully each party will think we're with the other one."

"Good idea." Neither of us has any idea how to do that, though, so we wind up standing in the middle of the room, slouching.

"Can I help you?" Mr. McAllister asks, coming out from behind the counter. He's wearing that same floppy hat that he's worn every time I've been here over the years.

"Um, we're looking for the magician?" Leo says.

Mr. McAllister points to a door marked PARTY ROOM where they usually serve the pizza and cake. "He's getting ready in there."

"Thanks," we say, and hurry toward the room before he can ask us any questions.

"Guess he didn't recognize us," Leo says.

"Amy and Leon, remember?"

"Right! Let's check on them."

He pulls me off to the side and I giggle when I realize where he's taking me. Next to the clown-shaped trampoline is a row of carnival mirrors. One makes you look tall and skinny, the other short and wide. We stand in front, expecting to see warped images of Leon and Amy. Only this time, two *other* strangers are reflected back at us! We both whirl around to look behind us, but we're alone in the hallway. I now have olive skin, long, shiny black hair, and am wearing cutoff shorts MUCH shorter than my mom would ever allow me out of the house in. I instinctively try to pull them down, but wind up grabbing my own jeans. The shorts do get a little longer, though. I move to check out Leo. He is now a bit plump with very short brown hair. If we look like this now, I wonder what — or who — we looked like at the beach! I run my hand over my new silky hair, only I still feel my own puffy hair instead. Not fair.

Suddenly I'm not alone in my mirror. "Funny!" Connor says, tugging at the corners of his mouth with his fingers. His reflection stretches two feet wide. Leo and I step to the side so he can have the whole mirror to himself. He wiggles and dances around in the mirror. That kid is not shy.

"Hey," Leo says, forcing his eyes away from his reflection, "I know it's your sister's birthday, but I have these really cool new video games. Do you want to play them? You can go sit over there if you want." He points to a bench on the other side of the room from Grace's party.

"Thanks, man," ten-year-old Connor says, "but there's a magician! They rock!"

I guess video games can't compare to a real live magician.

"Plan B," Leo says.

We leave Connor at the mirrors and hurry over to the party room. The magician is your typical party magician — black cape, top hat, podium with various tricks piled on it. When he hears us come in, he looks up from detangling three metal rings. "I'll be ready in five," he says.

"That's okay," Leo says. "We just wanted to tell you that the brother of the birthday girl is going to try to steal your rabbit."

He looks amused. "Is that so? He can have her as far as I'm concerned."

"What?" I ask, sure I'd heard him wrong.

He gestures under the podium at a pudgy bunny curled up in another slightly larger top hat. "She might look cute, but she's a little terror, that one."

The bunny's orange ears sway with each sleepy breath. "She doesn't look very scary."

"That's how they suck you in," he explains. "I've got another show tomorrow, but I might set her free in the woods afterward." Then, so quickly I almost miss it, he pulls off his hat and slips the bunny right inside the larger one. Then he puts the whole thing back on his head. The bunny is now hidden between the smaller hat and the bigger one. And this isn't a tiny bunny.

"So that's how they do that trick!" Leo says, leaning up to touch the brim of the magician's hat. You can't even tell it's really two hats anymore. There must be some kind of spring inside that releases the top of the smaller hat so the bunny can be pulled out.

"Shh," the magician says, batting his hand away. "Trade secret. Pretend you didn't see that."

I have to believe he's joking about leaving the bunny in the woods. "We're serious," I tell him. "You won't want to pick the red-haired boy to do any tricks."

He tips his hat at us and wheels his podium from the room.

"Plan C," Leo says. I nod, not happy about it. Plan C is my least favorite.

Grace's guests are now all sitting in rows, waiting for him to start, including Connor. We go all the way into the back to watch, careful not to block the tripod that holds up Mr. Kelly's video camera. The magician sets up his props in front of a banner that reads: THE AMAZING ZORO. He jumps right into his routine, making the kids laugh and clap. He calls Grace up to help with a disappearing milk trick. It's so weird watching her get tinier and tinier each year. Seven now, she could easily be mistaken for a five-year-old. She is still full of personality, though, laughing and joking.

"He's good," I whisper to Leo as the milk disappears as soon as Grace pours it into the jug.

Leo shrugs. "Not as good as Marvin the Magnificent."

"Who?"

"The magician we had for our fourth birthday party! Anyone can pull a rabbit from a hat. Marvin had a bird! Those things are unpredictable."

I smile, touched by the fact that he still remembers our fourth birthday.

The magician gets a round of applause for cutting a rope in half and then making it whole again. We know from the video that the rabbit trick comes up pretty quickly in the routine. Now that I saw how the trick is done, I'm glad he doesn't wait too long. I didn't see any holes poked in that hat.

I lean close to Leo and whisper, "Do you think that he was serious about letting her go in the woods?"

"I'm sure he was kidding."

"But what if he wasn't? She could starve in the woods."

"That bunny looked like she could miss a few meals and still be fine."

"What if she got eaten by wolves?"

"No wolves in Willow Falls. Get ready, the trick is up next."

The magician finishes pulling a dozen colored scarves out of a giggling girl's ear and asks if there are any volunteers to help him pull a rabbit from his hat. According to Plan C, this is when we're supposed to wave our hands wildly in the air and beg for him to pick one of us. It occurs to me that if we just let Connor steal the bunny, at least she would be safe. But as much as I don't want to leave the bunny with the magician, I want to heal Grace a lot more. So I join Leo as we wave our hands wildly. "Pick me! Pick me!" we shout.

I hear a few whispers of "Who *are* those people?" but we keep it up. Conner gets picked anyway. We watch him bound up to the front, all smiles and anticipation. It might be my imagination, but I think the magician winked in our direction.

"All right, young man," the magician says, "I'm going to wave my magic wand three times over this hat, which you can see is empty, correct?"

"Sure is," Connor says, peeking in.

"And then you're going to say *abracadabra* and pull out the cutest little bunny you ever did see. Are you ready?"

"Ready!"

The magician waves his wand three times and then points it at Connor.

"Abracadabra!" Connor shouts. He reaches in and pulls out the bunny. Everybody claps as he lifts her high with both hands.

The bunny doesn't even squirm. She just hangs there, wiggling her nose, her belly swaying gently. The magician holds out his hat for Connor to place the bunny back inside. Connor lowers the bunny halfway, then pauses, a look of mild confusion on his face.

"Just drop her on in, son," the magician says. But Connor doesn't let go. In fact, he lifts the rabbit back up and brings her close to his chest.

Mr. Kelly steps forward from the crowd. He tries to keep his voice light. "Put the rabbit back in the hat, Connor." When Connor refuses, Mr. Kelly grits his teeth. "Connor, you are being rude. Give the man his rabbit back."

"No," Connor says, first softly, then louder. "No! I'm not giving her back!" Then, as he did in the video, he runs right out the front door of Mr. McAllister's Magic Castle Birthday Party Palace, with his mom at his heels. Mr. Kelly hands the magician a twenty-dollar bill and tells him to keep going with the show. The magician tucks the bill into his pocket, looking not entirely unpleased. I shake my head at him as Leo and I slip out behind Mrs. Kelly.

"We simply can't keep her, Connor," Mrs. Kelly is saying when we get outside. We step a few feet away, checking our watches as though we are waiting for a ride.

"Grace is allergic to rabbit hair," she says. "Plus, since when did you become such a lover of rabbits? You didn't seem very interested at the county fair last spring."

"I just couldn't put her back in there," Connor says, still snuggling the bunny in his arms. "I don't trust him. And she's so roly-poly and cute, and her ears match my hair." He holds the bunny up next to his head. "See?"

While they argue over whether their hair is actually orange or red, Connor's grandfather gets out of a nearby car and sizes up the situation. "Kid stole the bunny, eh?" He speaks with a cool accent, like Irish maybe. I think Connor's family is from Ireland.

We nod. Leo says, "His dad tried to stop him, but he didn't listen."

"Cute little guy," the old man says, peering at the bunny.

"Actually," I say, "I think it's a girl."

He goes over to Connor and says, "I'm headed to the mall after this, and since you can't keep him, I can bring her to the pet shop for you."

Mrs. Kelly looks at Connor. "Is that okay, honey? Then the bunny will go to a good home."

"I guess so," Connor says, handing over the bunny.

His grandfather takes off his hat — which is brown and soft — and places the bunny inside. "I don't think this gal's fat. I'd bet she's in the family way."

"That means she's preggo," Leo whispers to me.

"I know what it means."

Mrs. Kelly leads Connor back inside and we watch as their grandfather heads to his car. The bunny peeks out from the top of the hat. She wiggles her nose, then opens her mouth wide and chomps down on the edge of the hat with surprising strength. When she sees us watching, she squints, almost like she's trying to wink, then dives in again for another bite.

"Okay, that bunny's a little weird," Leo says when we're alone in the parking lot. "So what do we do now? We don't really need to go back in. I don't even need to open the notebook to know we got a big X today."

I frown and then try to look on the positive side. "Hey, we helped save a bunny's life today. And a bunch of soon-to-be-born baby bunnies."

"I'm pretty sure that won't impress Angelina." He looks at his watch. "We still have an hour."

"And we have our bikes."

"We could go spy on ourselves," he suggests.

I try to remember what I'd most likely be doing right now, about a month after our fight started. Probably banging on my drums in the basement, feeling sorry for myself. No one needs to see that. I shake my head. "It's probably too risky. But what if we go scout out tomorrow's party? It's at the Creative Kids pottery studio where you and I had our fifth birthday. This is where Angelina enchanted the candles, but Connor blew them out before the benediction had enough time to work. We could try to figure out how we're going to stop it."

"I wish we could just ask Connor why he keeps messing everything up," Leo mutters.

"I know, it's very weird."

We're silent for a moment, and then Leo says, "Hey, we could get those trick candles that are really hard to blow out! Then when Connor tries, he won't be able to! That might buy us enough time for the benediction to work!"

We high-five. "Excellent thinking, Leon!"

"You, too, Amy!"

It takes only ten minutes to ride our bikes to the pottery store. It's funny seeing old ads in store windows and even some stores that don't exist anymore. The movie showing at the theater is three years old, which I know shouldn't surprise me, yet somehow still does.

The pottery store is empty except for a woman wiping down the tables. "Pick any piece from the shelf," she tells us. "The prices are on the bottom. Then you can choose your paint colors from the back."

"Oh, we're not . . ." Leo begins.

"Thanks," I say. "We'll look around." I lead him toward the pottery-filled shelves and whisper, "We can't just hang out without painting something. It would look suspicious."

He nods, then scans the shelves, picking up pieces and putting them back down. "This stuff is pricey."

I pick up one of a dancer. "We can make this one for Grace. It reminds me of her dancing in the play last week."

"I think she was mostly running in circles," Leo says. "How about this for Connor?" He holds up a rabbit with a carrot in its mouth.

"Perfect. Even though we can't tell him why we got it for him!" We set ourselves up at a table and go to the back to get the paint. While we're there we find a bathroom and a small supply room, with a back entrance. That could come in handy.

We set to work. I give my dancer Grace's red hair, and Leo gives the bunny orange ears so she looks like the one Connor rescued.

"As you know," Leo says, dabbing some pink on the nose, "I wrote my first poem about a bunny. 'Bunny, bunny, hop hop hop. White and soft like a little mop.'"

"Wow, that's bad."

"Hopefully I've gotten better." He checks his watch. "We better hurry. Getting stuck in the past would be a huge inconvenience."

We finish up and bring them to the counter. "We're done," Leo announces.

"That was fast," she says, ringing us up. Leo pays. She hands him the receipt and says, "Just bring this back with you in a few days and your pieces will be ready."

"Um, we can't take them with us?" I ask.

She shakes her head. "We have to glaze them and fire 'em in the kiln."

"Oh, right, I forgot." We reluctantly hand them over. At least they served as a good cover.

She consults a chart on the counter and says to herself, "Let's see, McKenna will be in tomorrow, Angelina's back in Thursday, then —"

"Wait, did you say Angelina?"

"Yes. Angelina D'Angelo. Do you know her?"

Leo and I exchange a look. "I only thought she pretended to work here for our party!"

"Me, too!" Leo turns back to the woman. "She actually works here?"

She nods. "Twice a week, going on five years now. She'd be here today, but she takes off for her birthday each year."

It's a good thing we're standing on the other side of the room from the shelves of fragile pottery, because both of us stagger backward. "Today is Angelina's birthday? Like, today, July fourteenth?"

She nods, giving us a strange look. "Are you friends of hers?"

"Yes," Leo says before I can even recover. He slaps his forehead. "But we forgot to get her a gift! Do you know if she still lives in those apartments on Maple?"

The woman shakes her head. "No, she's on Elm. Been there forever, I think. Never actually been invited there myself."

"Oh, right, Elm," Leo says. "I knew it was one of the trees. C'mon, Amy, we better hurry."

I let him drag me out of the store. We hop on our bikes and ride till we're out of earshot. "Something's not right," he says.

"I know! Angelina just forgets to mention that she and Grace have the same birthday? Angelina is ALL ABOUT BIRTHDAYS! Do you think it could just be a coincidence?"

But as soon as I say it, I know of course that it isn't. At the same time we both say, "There *are* no coincidences in Willow Falls."

Chapter Thirteen

We arrive back at Mr. McAllister's Magic Castle Birthday Party Palace with only a few minutes to spare. When the cars fade away and the music inside cuts off, we pedal at top speed back to the diner. Tara and Rory are waiting for us right in front. When they see us approaching, they run up. "Guess what?" the four of us shout at the same time. Then we laugh. "You first," I offer.

"Angelina's birthday is the same as Grace's!" Tara says.

"That's what *we* were going to tell *you*! How'd you find out?"

She waves a red envelope in her hand. "I found this by Angelina's chair after the bar mitzvah. When Rory and I went looking for her, I remembered I had it." She slips the card out of the envelope. "It was already opened, so I thought it would be okay to peek, like maybe it would give us some kind of clue as to where she went."

She hands it across to us. Leo takes it and I lean over to read it. On the front is a heart with the words BE MY VALENTINE on it. "Just open it," Tara says before I can question the fact that it's clearly a Valentine's Day card.

Leo opens it and reads, "Happy birthday to my dearest Angelina, you get more beautiful with each passing year." His eyebrows rise at that one, but he continues reading. "Today is the day we've been waiting for. I know you'll do the right thing. Our time is now." He looks up. "I don't get it."

I take the card from him and turn it over. "It's not signed. If we knew who it was from, we could try to find him."

"We *do* know who it's from!" Rory says.

"Bucky Whitehead gave it to her!" Tara shouts.

"Bucky?" Leo and I exclaim at the same time. I drop the card in surprise. Tara picks it up and slips it back in the envelope.

"Our Bucky, who we hang out with at the community center?" Leo asks.

"Bucky who was the fiddler in the play?" I ask. "Tall, white hair, that Bucky?"

Tara laughs. "Is there any other Bucky?"

"Bucky has a thing for Angelina? Seriously? How do you know it's from him?"

"Remember how I had to promise to run errands for him in exchange for him giving us his violin for Angelina's list?"

I nod.

"Well, one of the errands was to pick up this card! Correct me if I'm wrong, but if the magical stuff you guys went through with Angelina was on your eleventh birthday, and Rory's was on her twelfth, and mine was on my thirteenth, then having Grace turn ten the same day that Angelina has her *own* birthday — well, as one wise girl named Rory once told me, there are no coincidences in Willow Falls."

Rory laughs. "It was Leo who told *me* that."

"It's becoming more true every day," I say.

"I guess you didn't find Angelina?" Leo asks.

Rory shakes her head. "After Tara remembered the card, we went looking for Bucky, too. Apparently half the senior citizens in town went to a bridge tournament. They'll be back the day after tomorrow. We checked for Angelina everywhere that we could think of. We have no idea where she lives, though."

I grab her arm in excitement. "We do now!" I'd nearly forgotten that Leo had managed to uncover her address! "She lives somewhere on Elm!"

"No way!" Tara and Rory exclaim. "Angelina actually lives somewhere! Like a normal person! So weird!"

"I know! I think I've seen that street out by the mall. It's too far to ride on our bikes, though."

"We can ask Ray to take us in the morning," Tara suggests.

"Hey, you didn't say how it went at the party today," Rory says. "Two down, one to go?"

Leo and I shake our heads. "Big red X," Leo says. "We did get to scout out tomorrow's place, though, and we already have a plan."

"Which one's tomorrow?" Rory asks.

"It's at the paint-your-own-pottery place," I reply. "Connor blows out the candles and ruins the party."

"Conner, again?" Tara asks. "I didn't want to say it before, but seriously, maybe you should ask him why he messed up all his sister's birthday parties."

"I know," I say, "but how could we do that without him getting suspicious?"

"I'm pretty sure that his first guess wouldn't be that you're going back in time and watching them happen," Rory says.

"But what if he figures out I stole the videos then?" Leo asks.

"I'm sure he won't," Tara says.

"You're right," Leo says proudly. "I'm too good at my job."

I roll my eyes. "All right, if I can work it into the conversation, I will."

"So what did you find at the pottery store?" Rory asks.

"We found a back room where they'll probably keep the cake. There won't be any place for us to stay during the party, so we'll have to watch from outside. And we painted some pottery for Connor and Grace."

"Too bad we'll never see those pieces again," Leo says. "And mine was pretty good. Sort of good. Okay, it was pretty bad."

"Why won't you see them again?" Rory asks.

"Because we had to leave them in the past to get glazed," I explain. "We can't go back to the same year twice."

"You don't need to go back in time," she says. "The store's right around the corner."

"What do you . . . oh! You think they might still have them? After three years?"

She shrugs. "It's worth a try."

All our phones ding with texts at the same time. (Well, not Rory's. Her phone is so basic that it takes forever for her to write back, so no one texts her unless they don't mind waiting forever for an answer. She actually has to press each key a certain number of times per letter. It's barbaric.) The text is from Connor, telling us that Grace is ready for visitors now if we want to stop by.

Leo replies and says that we'll be there very soon.

"Will you guys let me know how she is?" Rory asks. "I have to go with my mom to check out places for Sawyer's birthday dinner next week. As he gets older it gets harder to find places he's not banned from!"

We promise to fill her in and then try not to laugh at Tara as she climbs onto the bubble-gum-pink bike that she's been borrowing from her cousin Emily. It's WAY too small for her. Tara sees our expressions and holds her head high. "Obviously you two are jealous of this fine machine."

"I'm definitely jealous of the tassels on the handlebars," Leo says.

"I'm jealous of the stickers on that banana seat," I add. "But seriously, that bike is much closer to my size. You take mine." I wheel it over to her.

"Are you sure?"

"Yup. I've always wanted a banana seat. You don't see those much anymore." We trade, and Tara looks much more comfortable. Since the pottery store is on the way, we decide to stop there first. The woman behind the counter looks pretty much the same as when we saw her less than an hour ago, except for her clothes and a few more gray hairs. Leo places the receipt on the counter. "We'd like to pick these up."

She takes a look at it, then peers closer. "Is this right? You made these three years ago? You certainly kept the receipt in excellent condition."

She's right; the paper doesn't even have a crease on it, and the ink isn't even dry.

"Time just flew by," Leo says.

She looks doubtful. "Well, we do have a bin in the back for unclaimed items. We can see if it's there." She leads us to the back room and slides a box out from below the counter.

"Have at it," she says, pushing the box toward us. Leo and I kneel down and pull out random pieces of pottery. Unicorns, Christmas ornaments, picture frames, bowls, and at the very bottom, a dusty rabbit and dancer tied together with a rubber band. Leo holds the small bundle aloft. "Success!"

Besides the videos changing, this is the first real, hold-in-your-hand proof that we have of visiting the past. Tara whistles. "That's pretty cool."

Leo wipes the dust off, and they shine much more than when we handed them in. The glaze really makes them look kind of nice. The woman wraps them in bubble wrap and I lay them in the basket of the banana bike and try not to go over too many bumps on the way to Grace's house.

I had expected the house to be really quiet like a hospital, but loud music reaches us as we climb up the porch steps. "The doctor said stimulation is good!" Mrs. Kelly shouts over the noise as she lets us in. "Connor's up with her now," she says. "Her friend Bailey just left. It's nice of you to want to support Connor. This is very hard for him. They're very close." Her eyes fill with tears. If Rory were here, she'd hug her. But since she isn't, I do it instead. She seems surprised but smiles at me as she points the way upstairs.

When we came here to gather Grace's stuff, I hadn't noticed the poster of *Playing It Cool* taped on her bedroom door. She drew antlers and a beard on Madison's face in red marker. I snap a picture of it with my phone to email Rory.

Tara knocks, and Connor swings open the door. "Hi, New Girl."

"Tara," she says, then slower, "Ta-ruh."

Connor shrugs. "I like *New Girl*."

"Yeah, whatever, that's fine." Tara pushes by him and goes over to the bed. It's much quieter in here. Just some soft music playing that sounds very familiar.

"Wait, is that from *Fiddler on the Roof*?" I ask. "Like, our actual production of it?"

He nods. "I made a recording from my dad's video. Since Friday was the last night she was . . . well, *normal*, we thought hearing the singing might help." He steps aside so we can get closer to the bed. Grace is propped up on pillows, and her eyes are open again. They still seem blank. A tube attached to her arm is feeding her a steady stream of clear liquid. Her face looks less pale, but the big change is in her hands. Her fingers are moving! They tap together, almost like she's knitting something, except there is no yarn. And no knitting needles. And she's not, like, an eighty-year-old grandmother. Still, it's a good sign, I think. At least I hope it is!

"I wanted to surprise you guys," Connor says when he sees our jaws fall open at the change in Grace. "She also talks a little."

"She does?" Tara asks, wide-eyed. This is the first time she's seen Grace in this state, but she is doing a good job at not staring. Well, not staring too much.

"Every few minutes, she comes out with these long bursts of words that don't make any sense. Just wait, you'll hear."

While we wait, I place the dancer on Grace's nightstand. "This made me think of her." I hand him the bunny statue. "And Leo made this one for you."

"For me?" Connor asks, taking it carefully from me. "A rabbit?"

"It reminded me of you," Leo says. At Connor's confused expression he explains, "Because of the orange ears. You know, your hair?"

"Cool. Thanks." He tilts the bunny back and forth in the light. "I feel like I've seen this guy before." He shrugs and sets it down on the dresser.

I take a deep breath. "Um, Connor," I begin, "can I ask you something?" Before he can answer or I can chicken out, I blurt out, "Did you and Grace always get along?"

"Yeah, pretty much. Why?"

"Um, this is going to sound strange, but this girl I babysit for was at one of Grace's birthday parties a few years ago. She said you leaned over and blew out the candles on Grace's cake before she could do it." I can't meet Connor's eyes. Now I'm going to have to find some girl from the party and see if her mom needs a babysitter so my story won't be a total lie!

Connor scratches his head. "I guess that could have happened. I'm not sure. It's very fuzzy. Like I think I remember doing it, but not *why* I would do it." He thinks for a minute, then gives a surprised laugh. "I'm pretty sure I also ran right into her birthday cake one year and toppled it over. And another time I sat on one of the presents and smashed it. I must have a jinx on me or something!"

Tara, Leo, and I don't dare look at one another. He might not be so far off. Maybe Angelina's enchantment leaked onto him somehow.

"But Grace never got mad at me," Connor says, looking down and patting her arm. The song that Connor and David performed together starts to play. He turns to Tara. "Hey, have you heard from the Hamburglar?"

"Bee Boy," I mutter, but they ignore me.

"Not since yesterday morning," Tara says quietly.

"Don't feel bad," Connor says. "It's like that when he goes to visit his dad. I think he feels like when he's there, he should be totally there, ya know?"

Tara nods. "I'm sure he —"

But she's cut off by Grace, who has begun to speak. We all hurry to the side of the bed, even though she's speaking very loudly.

"My boy first true love purple I'll pay whatever you ask gold and tree bark two pinches of tarragon and elderberries waxing moon my apples you lout!"

Then, just as quickly, the words stop and her face settles back into its usual expression. Upon closer examination, though, she looks slightly less amazed, a little more confused, and now there's something else mixed in — concentration and surprise?

"Does she always say the same things?" I ask.

He shakes his head. "Never the same. She reads a lot, so my mom thinks maybe she's saying things she remembers from books."

"When exactly did it start?" Leo asks.

Connor thinks for a minute. "I guess right around lunchtime yesterday."

Again we have to avoid making eye contact with each other or he's going to start to wonder if something's up. But maybe our theory was right, and fixing the beach party *did* have something to do with her change.

At that moment Grace bursts out laughing, like she's just heard the most hilarious thing in the world, then stops and resumes her silent staring and invisible knitting.

Connor sighs. "Oh, yeah, she does *that* now, too."

Chapter Fourteen

"You're sure this is the right way?" Ray asks. We don't answer because we're not sure. We passed the end of Elm Street about five minutes back. Now we're on a dirt road that as far as we can tell, just leads farther into the woods near Apple Grove. Over the last year that Leo and I have been working to bring the apples back to Apple Grove, we've never explored this area. I didn't even know the woods went back this far.

"Do you think we're lost?" Tara asks.

"Do you smell that?" Ray asks. He leans his head toward his open window.

"Apples!" we exclaim.

"We must be getting close," Rory says.

"You're officially one of us now, Ray," I tell him.

"Unless we just passed an apple tree," he replies.

"Oh, Ray," Tara says. "Have I taught you nothing? There are no more apple trees in Apple Grove. Well, except the little ones that don't make apples yet."

"Look!" Leo shouts from the front seat. "That's gotta be her house!"

Ray pulls to the side of the road. Even though it's half hidden by thick trees, the yellow three-story house could belong to no one else. With its white wicker shutters and wraparound porch, it almost looks like a house from a storybook. Herbs and flowers neatly divided into small gardens fill the front lawn, while a large birdbath sits directly in the middle. We pile out of the car and stop in front of the gate. A low wooden fence surrounds the entire property. We could easily step over it, but no one does.

A wooden sign staked into the ground warns, IF I DIDN'T INVITE YOU HERE, GO AWAY.

"Well, ya gotta hand it to her," Ray says. "She doesn't waste words. Guess we'll be going."

"No way," Leo says. "We came for answers." He reaches for the gate, which I fully expect to be locked or enchanted or something. But it swings open easily, without even a creak. He steps through and the rest of us start to follow.

"I'll just hang back here," Ray says. "You know, guard the periphery."

"You're sure?" Tara asks, holding the gate for him.

"Hey, anyone who can get people stuck in time and send people BACK in time ain't someone I need to mess with."

"Fair enough," she says.

It turns out he didn't need to worry because no one is answering the door. Leo keeps ringing the bell while Rory, Tara, and I wander through the lawn reading the names of herbs printed on little sticks. There are some really strange ones. Feverfew, coltsfoot, pennyroyal, fenugreek seed, marjoram, nettle. Some are only a few inches tall, others reach my knees. The gardens look very well kept, although nothing seems to have been cut recently.

I pass the birdbath (which is also a sundial) and join Leo on the porch. "Maybe she's still asleep? It's not even nine o'clock yet." We'd had to get an early start because the pottery party starts at ten.

"I don't think she's here," he says. "I guess *gone fishing* really means gone fishing. And the windows are tinted or something. I can't see inside at all."

I check the time on my phone. "We better go. We still have to pick up the trick candles at the drugstore." He knocks one more time and gives up. Tara looks up from a patch of tiny white flowers atop long green stems. The sign is labeled YARROW. "Look close," Tara says, pointing to the sign. Below the word *yarrow*, I can just make out the word *love* in tiny handwriting. "I think Angelina uses these to make potions."

Leo laughs. "I don't think Angelina's the potion-making type."

Tara shrugs and turns on her heel. "You don't know everything, Leo Fitzpatrick."

I laugh and nudge his arm. "She sure told you."

"I was going to bring you some candles," Rory says as we climb back in the car. "But my dad used them all up on his own birthday. He thinks they're hilarious."

"No wonder our dads were friends growing up," Tara says.

We arrive at the pottery store with only ten minutes to spare, so we'll have to buy the candles when we get to the past. Leo takes out his dollars and trades with Ray until he doesn't have any bills more recent than four years ago. He's good at remembering these little details.

The streets are pretty crowded as far as Willow Falls goes, so we decide to wait around the back of the store. "What do you guys see when we disappear?" I ask the others.

"We only saw it happen at the beach," Rory says. "It was superquick. Like, in a split second, you were just gone. Poof!"

"And no one else noticed?"

"Nope."

"Has Jake remembered anything about the time he was out?" Leo asks.

"I don't know," Rory says. "He's been so busy with publicity stuff for the movie that I've only gotten short emails."

"At least you know he's thinking about you," Tara says. "I still haven't heard from David. I'm a little worried. I mean, I know he's with his family, it's just, well, there's so much I've kept from him since I've been in town, like all the Angelina stuff, and everything about why I was sent here in the first place. Maybe he just got tired of not knowing what was going on."

"Okay," Ray says with a wave. "That's about as much teenage girl drama as I can handle. I'll meet those of you who don't disappear back at the car."

"Oh, sure," Leo calls after him. "Just leave me here all alone to represent our gender!"

"Sorry, Leo," Tara says. "We can talk about sports if you want. Go, team!"

"Listen, Tara, David's not mad about anything," he assures her. "Boys don't think about what girls are thinking. I'm sure he didn't even notice you were hiding anything. We're not that observant."

"Boys don't think about what girls are thinking?" I ask, hands on my hips.

"Yeah," Tara says. "I thought you were, like, this sensitive poet type."

Leo takes a step back as we all wait patiently for him to come up with an acceptable answer. He raises his wrist, points at his watch, and says, "See ya in four years."

But instead of us being the ones to disappear, it's Rory and Tara. I mean, I know it isn't really, but from where I'm standing, it looks that way. I quickly glance around to make sure we're alone. A squirrel jumps up from the curb and skitters away, but that's about it.

I reach out to the spot where they had been standing and wave my hand in the air. "So weird. It's like we know they're here, in the same space, just not the same time."

"I know, it's enough to drive you bonkers if you think about it too much. And you know us boys, not liking to think about stuff."

"Come, my sensitive poet, let's get to the drugstore before there's a last-minute run on trick candles." I grab his arm and we snake through the back alleys of the stores until there's no other choice but to go back onto Main Street. Even though we know we don't look like ourselves, it still feels risky to be out in public view like this. We keep our heads down and walk the next three blocks as quickly as we can.

The drugstore is unusually crowded. "What's with all these people?" Leo asks, pushing his way through the door. A lady on her way out points to a sign on the door. OUR TEN-YEAR-ANNIVERSARY SALE, EVERYTHING 20% OFF AND DOUBLE COUPONS!

I pull him off to the side, away from the lines at the register. "Let's just get in and get out, as Angelina would say."

"But what would Rory's mother say?"

"Huh?"

He turns me around until we are practically face-to-face with Rory's mother. I jump back and almost knock Leo into a display of lipsticks. Mrs. Swenson glances up, clutching a bright pink lipstick in one hand and a pile of coupons in the other. "Do you think this is a good color for me?" she asks, holding the lipstick up to her face. Without waiting for an answer, she says, "Too young looking? Yeah, you're right." I'm trying to shrink into the background but she must not notice because she holds the lipstick out to me. "Here. With your shade of strawberry blond and those cheekbones, this will look really pretty on you."

So I guess I'm strawberry blond today. With cheekbones. Doesn't everyone have cheekbones? When I don't move, Leo lifts my arm. Mrs. Swenson places the lipstick in my hand and takes off down the aisle.

Leo laughs at me. "You realize we barely even knew Rory four years ago. Even if we looked like ourselves, her mom wouldn't have known who we were."

"Yeah, yeah, it was still scary." I turn around to place the lipstick back on the shelf and catch sight of myself in the makeup mirror stuck on the wall. I gasp without meaning to. I'm *hot*! Like, supermodel hot. Well, I can only see my face, so I can't vouch for the rest of me, but there's not a single blemish on my skin and my silky hair falls in gentle waves over my shoulders.

Leo's eyes widen when he sees my reflection, then he shrugs. "I like you with freckles."

I shake my head. "You're crazy." I step aside and he takes my place.

"I'm Japanese!" he shouts, then quickly lowers his voice. "That is the coolest thing!"

"I love the scarf and the red tips on the ends of your hair," I say. "Very punk!" We admire him for another minute before two teenage girls elbow their way in front of the mirror. They both check him out, but he doesn't even notice. I pull him away possessively. A guy with an official badge around his neck walks by and I stop him to ask where to find the candles.

"Party supplies are at the end of the baby aisle," he says, pointing a few aisles away.

"Thanks," I tell him and drag Leo behind me.

"I can walk on my own, you know," he complains.

"You can't be trusted not to wander off. I know how you get in stores like this."

"Hey, that's not fair. It's not my fault my mom never took me shopping as a little kid." He imitates his mom's voice. "As famous philosopher Henry David Thoreau once wrote, 'That man is the richest whose pleasures are the cheapest.'" No sooner are the words are out of his mouth than I catch him looking longingly at a huge display of paper napkins.

"Your mom still makes you reuse yours till it falls apart?"

"Uh-huh."

"That's pretty gross."

"Uh-huh."

I drag him away and we turn into the baby aisle. We have to step around a girl in pigtails. Her baby brother is gleefully flinging pacifiers at shoppers' legs while his sister struggles to take them from him and put them back in the bucket they came from. I'm glad I don't have any younger siblings. Not that having an older one is such a joy, but still, it's hard enough to be responsible for myself, let alone a little kid.

I bend down to help the girl pick them up.

"Thanks," she says, pushing up the glasses that have slipped down her nose. "The second my dad went to grab something at the end of the aisle, my brother decided to do this. I think he lives to embarrass me. And he's not even one yet!"

She smiles gratefully as I hand her a bunch of pacifiers and I realize she's older than I first thought — she's just small and her hairstyle makes her look even younger. Leo yanks my arm so tight, I'm afraid he's going to pull it right off. "Don't talk to her!" he hisses in my ear. "That's Rory!!"

I whirl back around. The girl is bending down again because this time her brother has torn open a box of Cheerios. I gasp for the second time in as many minutes. He's totally right! *It's nine-year-old Rory!* We should keep moving, but we're trapped by shoppers on both sides, and I kind of want to stare at this version of Rory for a few seconds longer.

"Look what I found!" Mr. Swenson calls out, pushing his way through the aisle.

"Guess the whole family's here," Leo mutters.

Mr. Swenson holds up his basket. "Trick candles! They'll be perfect for Sawyer's birthday party next week. He'll never see it coming! I grabbed all the ones they had!"

"That's great, Dad," Rory says. "A little help here?"

"Hang on a few more minutes, hon. Your mom gave me a whole list. You're doing great."

Before she can complain again, he takes off. I can't help but notice there is no stripe in his hair yet.

Leo hisses at me again. "He took all the candles!"

"I know," I whisper back. "We can't exactly tackle him."

"C'mon, Sawyer," Rory says, turning back to her brother. "Let's find a more boring aisle with nothing to play with." She reaches down to pick him up and then quickly straightens up again. I expect to see Sawyer in her arms, but they're empty.

I look down. Sawyer's not there! I turn around in a circle. He must have crawled through people's legs in the split second Rory was talking to their father. Instead of freaking out like I thought she would, Rory merely sighs and shuts her eyes. I'm about to offer to help find him when I hear a whistle blow. Rory opens her eyes. "And there it is," she says, taking off in the direction of the whistle. We hurry after her.

"You can't do that, little boy!" the store manager is yelling. "That's for display purposes only!" We round the corner to find Sawyer, pants and diaper at his ankles, sitting on a plastic Elmo potty in the middle of aisle three. He looks up and gives Rory a big grin and two thumbs up.

The manager is turning all sorts of unpleasant shades of red. Rory's parents arrive and take in the scene. Mrs. Swenson hands her husband her fistful of coupons and bends down for Sawyer. "Look on the bright side, honey," Mr. Swenson says as Mrs. Swenson pulls up Sawyer's pants. "I bet he'll be really easy to toilet train!"

"You know you're buying that now," the manager says, barely containing his anger.

"We've gotta go," Leo whispers as Rory's dad assures the manager that Elmo will be going home with them. Leo drags me away from the scene, which really, in any other circumstances, would have had us laughing until our sides hurt. We turn into the much less crowded greeting card aisle, where he lifts the bottom of his shirt and quickly drops it again, but not before I could see the box of trick candles stuck in his waistband!

"Where did you . . ." I lower my voice. "You're not going to steal those!"

"Of course not," he says, pulling the box out. "I mean, I did steal them from Rory's dad's basket when he was otherwise occupied with a peeing baby, but c'mon, the guy had six boxes. That's called being greedy."

"Slick move, Leon," I say as he strides up to the last aisle, which fortunately is the farthest from where Mrs. Swenson is now trying to convince the manager to sell them the potty at a discount since it's used. Mr. Swenson doesn't seem to notice that his basket is one box of candles lighter. We pay and run out of the store, not looking back. We only slow down when we get within a few stores of the pottery place. I lean against the wall to catch my breath. "Do you think Rory will remember me, I mean *Amy*, talking to her?"

"I'm not sure. Depends on how many embarrassing moments she's had. This one might not stand out."

I consider this. She's had a lot just in the last few years that we've been friends. And this one clearly wasn't the first. Even though it was risky talking to her, it was really cool and I'm totally glad I did it.

Leo and I slip around the back of the pottery store. The back door is open, with just a screen door between us and the party that we can hear going on inside. The door creaks as we open it, but it's way too loud in there for anyone to notice. As we'd hoped, the cake is sitting on the counter in the back room. Beside it lays a box of small pink candles.

I reach into the bag from the drugstore and pull out the new ones. Besides being rainbow colored, our candles are considerably taller. "What are we going to do?"

"We don't have a choice," Leo says, already shoving the pink box into his pocket. "Let's just leave them here. Maybe they won't notice."

I place ours on the counter. "Or maybe they'll think the store gives everyone a free box."

We slip back out, then hurry around to the front so we can watch through the store window. It takes a while to collect all the pottery pieces and clean off the tables so Mrs. Kelly can lay out the paper plates. Leo already has Angelina's notebook out in front of him, staring down at the page. "Any minute now," he says.

The singing begins and we risk pressing our faces up to the glass. I'm very relieved to see our candles in the cake, their tiny flames dancing and sparkling. "We didn't leave them much choice," Leo whispers, reading my mind.

Grace makes her wish, then begins to blow out the candles. As expected, Connor squeezes right up next to her and blows as hard as he can. The flames flicker and we grab each other's hands tight. But the flames soon return, strong as ever. Everyone laughs and Mr. Kelly forcibly removes Connor from the table. Grace giggles and keeps huffing and puffing until all of them are out. All the kids and grown-ups are laughing and clapping with delight. I glance over at Connor. He just seems confused. Only two grown-ups aren't laughing — Mrs. Kelly, who is busy glaring at Connor for trying to blow out his sister's candles, and their grandfather, who is frowning at a piece of broken pottery in his hand.

"Ta-da!" Leo says, holding up the notebook. "A big red check mark!" We high-five and run around to the back of the store again. One of the college girls who they hired to help with the party is carrying some trash out to the dumpster. If she doesn't get back in on time, she's going to see us disappear!

She turns back toward the building, but then stops and takes out her phone. My heart sinks. "What do we do?"

"I got us out of this before," Leo says confidently. "I can do it again."

We walk over to the spot where we first arrived, and even though I'm sure she must be wondering why we're standing here, she's too absorbed in her conversation to say anything. She's still only a few feet away from us, though. This is not good.

I lean toward him and whisper, "I think she's too old to care if Jake Harrison was spotted nearby."

"I got this, don't worry." Leo checks his watch. "Okay, here goes nothing."

I take a deep breath and cross my fingers. "Hey!" Leo shouts at the girl. "Is that a chicken?" She looks over at us and then at the dumpster behind her where Leo is pointing.

The next thing I know we're flying ten feet in the air.

Chapter Fifteen

I land on my butt. I have just enough time to register that it doesn't hurt as much as I thought it would before I bounce right back up again. I finally come to rest, staring up at the wide blue sky above. Leo's sneaker is tangled in my hair and I think my pinky might have gone in his ear. "Seriously, guys? A trampoline?" I turn my head toward my so-called friends.

Ray, Tara, and Rory are literally pounding the ground, they are laughing so hard.

"We couldn't help it," Tara said, gasping for breath. "It's so boring waiting for you to come back."

"You should have seen your faces." Rory wipes tears from her eyes. "It was all Ray's idea."

"You're a grown man, Ray," I remind him. "Or you know, mostly grown. I would have expected more from you."

Ray shakes his head, trying to look serious. This would be easier if he weren't clutching his belly and shaking with laughter. He takes deep breaths until he's able to speak. "All I did was drag it from the sporting goods store down the street."

Leo groans and rolls over. "There *is* no sporting goods store down the street."

"Hmm, it did look suspiciously like someone's backyard," Ray admits. "Either way, I'll return it. Don't be wowsers, it was ace!"

I'm pretty sure we've just been insulted. "So glad we could entertain you." I untangle Leo's shoe and toss it to him.

Leo tries to push himself to a sitting position but winds up springing forward onto his face. The others stifle a laugh. "Why does my ear hurt?"

"Sorry 'bout that," I say, rolling to the edge. I know better than to try to sit up or walk. Once I reach it, Rory pulls me off.

"You're not really mad, are you?" she asks.

"I guess it was better than landing in a hole full of sand again." I take out my phone — which fortunately bounced along with the rest of me — and call Connor to see if Grace has improved. The call goes to voice mail, so I leave a message and then text just to be sure.

Ray and Leo half drag, half carry the trampoline back to its rightful place while Tara and Rory and I head over to the pizza place down the street. We grab sodas from the case and pick a big table in the front. I want to find out if Rory remembers seeing me in the past but don't want to ask outright, in case it messes something up in the space-time continuum. Not that I know what that is, but it's something I heard on *Star Trek* once when my dad was watching a weekend-long marathon, and it sounds like something you should avoid doing.

So I try to be really vague and tell them that the drugstore was really busy and at first we couldn't find the candles, but then some kid distracted everyone and we were able to get the last box. Rory listens to the story with a look of growing unease on her face. I continue the story and may have let slip that there was a plastic Elmo potty involved. Then her eyes open wide as the realization hits her.

"Was that *you* who helped me with Sawyer? Were you really pretty? I mean, not that you're not pretty now, of course, but —"

"You two saw each other?" Tara asks, clearly confused. "But Rory was here the whole time."

I look around the restaurant to see if time is going to fold in on itself or something, but nothing seems to change. "Leo and I saw the nine-year-old version of her." I lean over and pinch Rory's cheek. "And she was so cute!"

Rory bats my hand away playfully. "I wasn't wearing pigtails, was I?"

"Do you want me to lie?" I ask. "Seriously, you were adorable and so was Sawyer."

She closes her eyes. "I can't believe he peed in that potty."

Tara giggles and says, "Sorry I missed that."

Ray and Leo join us. "Sorry you missed what?" Ray asks.

"Rory's little brother peeing in the middle of the drugstore," Tara says.

He wrinkles his nose. "Glad to have sat that one out. Will you guys manage without me for a bit? I have to help the boss strip the rubber off two hundred old tires."

Leo opens his mouth but Ray holds up his hand. "Don't even ask, because I have no idea. When you work for an inventor, you never know what they're cooking up."

We assure him we will survive without his supervision. At least until the next time we need a ride.

Time travel really does make a person hungry! I've eaten two slices and am on to my third when Connor returns my call. I put my phone on speaker so we can all hear.

"You won't believe what happened," he says as soon as I say hello.

"Is she better?" I ask. "Is she talking more?"

"She's not talking at all anymore, actually."

The four of us exchange disappointed looks. Even Leo puts down his slice.

"But wait till I tell you this!" We hear a deep intake of breath, then, "Grace grew four inches!"

"What?" we all shout at once, causing a few other customers to turn and look our way. I quickly take the phone off speaker and hold it to my ear. "Let me get this straight. Your sister grew four inches taller since we saw her yesterday?"

"No, not since yesterday," he says. "Since an hour ago! Seriously, it just happened. She usually grows, like, an inch a year, not even. It's like she grew four years' worth, instantly!"

"We'll be there in five minutes."

It takes closer to ten, but we're soon standing by her bedside. Flowers and balloons now cover every available surface. Her parents, the gray-haired doctor from the hospital, and another man in a baseball cap whisper in the corner. I recognize the younger man as Dr. Frieling, my pediatrician.

"It's Dr. Frieling's day off, but he came by to see her," Connor explains. "He's the one who noticed first. Come look."

We step closer and right away I can tell she looks different. The sleeves of her shirt are really tight, and her sweatpants are almost at her knees.

"Where's the IV?" I ask.

"She doesn't need it anymore!" Connor says. "She's able to eat and drink now."

I look up at Grace's face. Her expression hasn't changed much. She's still not blinking. "And you said she's not saying all those words anymore?"

He shakes his head. "I guess that's a good thing. She's not laughing anymore, either, though." He smiles wistfully. "I liked that part."

Dr. Frieling tips his cap at me as Mr. Kelly leads him out. I glance down, suddenly shy. It's weird seeing your doctor in the real world. The doctor from the hospital leaves, too, after handing a long list of instructions to Mrs. Kelly. She lays them on the nightstand next to my statue of the dancer.

"It's so kind of you to visit again," she says. "Have you seen our latest miracle? Four inches! Grace is going to be pretty surprised when she wakes up." She blinks away a tear. "*If* she wakes up."

Connor puts his arm around his mom. "Of course she will, Mom. Look how far she's come since Saturday."

"I could bring some clothes," Rory offers. "Looks like she can use a bigger size."

"That would be wonderful," Mrs. Kelly says, squeezing Rory's shoulder.

"I should have some, too," I say. "And probably some shoes."

"I hadn't even thought about her feet," Mrs. Kelly says, going down to inspect them. She smiles and tickles the bottom. We all look up at Grace's face to see how she'll react.

No response. Mrs. Kelly's smile fades. She mumbles, "Thank you," again, and hurries from the room. Connor casts us an apologetic look and follows her out.

"Hey," Tara says brightly. "Look at it this way. By this time tomorrow, Grace could be totally normal again. Only one more check mark to go, and how hard can it be to keep one eight-year-old boy from knocking over a cake?"

Leo grimaces. "We're not above tackling him at this point."

I stand beside Grace and take a good look. "Seriously, guys, I think this is what she would look like now if Angelina had been able to give her the benediction when she was born. Like we've given her two-thirds of it now by saving two out of three birthdays."

"I think you're right," Rory says. "I mean, I know I'm small for my age, but not like Grace was."

"Angelina told us Grace had all these stomach problems when she was really young that kept her from growing as well as other kids. She wouldn't have had those problems if Angelina hadn't failed."

"Well, let's get her some clothes that fit so she's more comfortable," Rory says. "We'll need to call one of our parents for a ride. Who will ask the fewest questions? My dad's at work and asking my mom means we get Sawyer, too. And you know how unpredictable that can be."

"Mine are both at work," Leo says.

"My mom's decorating a house across town," I say. "She'd probably be able to take a break if we needed her to, though."

"I'll call my mom," Tara says. "She'll ask a lot of questions and will totally embarrass me, but I can live with it. Plus I think she really likes driving around in my aunt's car."

Not even five few minutes later, a large silver SUV careens into the driveway. "That was really fast," Leo says as we head to the car. "Your mom must have broken all sorts of traffic laws."

We pile into Tara's aunt's huge car and I can't help but notice that Mrs. Brennan looks like a kid in the driver's seat. Tara definitely gets her height from her dad.

"Where to?" she asks, smiling at each of us. Rory gives directions and we head toward the other side of town at a normal, safe speed. Mrs. Brennan keeps grinning. She's even bouncing in her seat a little.

"Are you really this excited to be driving carpool, Mom?" Tara asks.

Rory leans forward. "Maybe you drank too much coffee, Mrs. B. That happened to me once."

Tara's mom laughs. "Nope. I ran into an old friend today. My best friend, actually. From when I was your age. I thought she'd never talk to me again. But she did."

Tara's eyes widen. "Polly?"

Her mom nods. "Yup. I'm going to show her the new house today."

"That's so great," Tara says, beaming.

"I'll have to work hard to earn her trust back, but at least she's letting me try." Then she glances at us in the rearview mirror. "So, what did you guys do today?"

No one rushes to answer her. I feel like I should say something so as not to be rude, but somehow the words *We went back in time four years, met one of our best friends when she*

*was nine, stopped a kid from blowing out his sister's candles,
which somehow made her grow four inches, and then landed on
a trampoline* have trouble leaving my mouth.

"Nothing much," Tara finally says. "Oh, we had pizza!"

Mrs. Brennan slows down, then pulls over to the curb and
stops the car.

"Um, my house is still a few blocks away," Rory says.

Mrs. Brennan turns so she's facing all of us. "Did Tara tell
you what I did when I was a little older than you guys?"

Surprised at her question, we all shake our heads.

"Mom!" Tara says. "Can we talk about this later?"

Her mother thinks for a minute. "All right, then, I'll just say
this. I know when Angelina D'Angelo is involved with something. I can smell it."

Leo sniffs under his arms. "You can?"

I elbow him in the ribs.

"Okay, not literally," she says. "But I can sense it. I think
anyone who has had dealings with her in the past can recognize
others caught in the middle of it."

We all nod in agreement. Amanda and I had seen it in Rory
last year, and this summer we all saw it in Tara. I lean forward
in my seat. "You knew her when you lived here?"

She nods. "And then after I left, too. It may start out with
her trying to help, but I fear the only person Angelina's really
looking out for is herself."

Wow. I may not always be Angelina's biggest fan, but gener-
ally I think her heart is in the right place. Tara's mom must
have had a really hard time. No wonder Tara hasn't wanted to
talk about it yet. If ever.

"Mom, we're just trying to help a friend," Tara says. "It's almost over."

"You might be right, Tara," her mom says. "But trust me, Angelina only lets you see what she wants you to see, and it's never the whole picture."

"You said it, sistah," Rory says as the rest of us nod in agreement. Seemingly satisfied, Mrs. Brennan continues the drive to Rory's house. But her warning echoes in my ears the rest of the day.

Chapter Sixteen

"*I feel good about this,*" *Leo says as we walk down* the street toward Grace's house. "I think this is our last trip back."

"I hope you're right." The street is quiet in the middle of the day, which is always helpful when you're about to vanish. Grace's fifth birthday party was held in her backyard, and it took repeated viewings of the video to figure out a halfway decent excuse for us to be there. The video didn't reveal how or why Connor happened to wind up on top of the cake, but it did show him being sent to his room to "think about what he'd done."

Basically, our plan is to wait for the pizza delivery guy to arrive. When he does, we'll give him ten bucks to let us bring the pizza around to the party in the backyard. We don't have much of a plan after that, but at least it gets us there.

"It seems like we only get to be alone together when we go back in time," Leo says. "I mean, I like our friends, of course, but I like being alone with you more." He reaches for my hand. We haven't held hands in a few days and I'm afraid it's going to feel weird, but it doesn't. It feels nice.

"Kylie told me no one stays with their first boyfriend," I blurt out.

He frowns. "How would Kylie know that?"

I shrug. "She's had a lot of boyfriends. I guess you learn stuff."

"We'll have to prove her wrong, then." He grips my hand even tighter.

We're still a few minutes early and don't want to risk Connor or his parents noticing us and inviting us inside. "Over there," Leo says, pointing to a bench on the side of a house across the street. "We should still be close enough to the party to slip back in time when it starts."

He was right. I know this because less than a minute after we sit down, the bench disappears beneath us and we fall right onto our butts. Five seconds after that, a stream of water from a nearby sprinkler hits us both directly in the face. Rory and Tara would have loved it.

I sputter and crawl out of the way before the sprinkler can swing back around and get us again. Leo crawls over to me. "Guess that bench wasn't here six years ago."

"Guess not," I reply, wiping my face with my sleeve. "Think we'll laugh about this someday?"

"I'm already laughing on the inside," he says, wiping his check with his hand. He only succeeds in making it messier by smearing mud on his nose. I can't help laughing as I do my best to clean him up with my shirt. He does the same for me. By the time the pizza delivery car pulls up at the curb, we're as presentable as we're gonna get. "Showtime," Leo says, pulling me up.

The delivery guy is lifting a pile of pizza boxes off of his passenger seat when we arrive at his side. "Hi," I say with a little wave. "Can we, um, help with those?" Leo holds out the ten-dollar bill. The guy looks from the money to the receipt taped to the top box in the pile and then at us. "The bill is for sixty-four dollars," he says, holding out his hand.

Leo lays the ten on the guy's palm. "How about we give you this, and you let us carry the boxes to the backyard."

The guy shrugs and stuffs the bill in his pocket. "Whatever floats your boat." He hands me two boxes and Leo three, leaving his own arms free. He swings them and whistles as we all trudge to the backyard together.

The party is in full swing already. Tables and chairs dot the lawn with a few umbrellas for shade. Kids splash and shout in wading pools, while the parents keep one eye on their kids and try to have a real conversation at the same time. This is the first of Grace's parties where the parents of the kids attending it came, too. I guess because the kids are so young. At five, Grace is so cute I can't even stand it.

"You can put those over here," Mrs. Kelly instructs us, pointing to a long table draped with a pink-and-white-checkered tablecloth.

We lay the boxes on the table and back away while she pays the real delivery guy. Trying to blend into the crowd isn't going to work. There's no one between the ages of six and thirty except Connor and one other boy around the same age. The boy has spiky brown hair and is currently standing very close to his mom, who is talking with Mr. Kelly. We'd seen him in the video but hadn't paid any attention, figuring he was a cousin or neighbor. But something about the way he's squinting up at his mom while she's talking feels familiar. I grip Leo's arm. "That's *David*!"

Leo takes a few steps closer to him. "You're right! I bet he just moved here."

We watch as Mr. Kelly waves for Connor to come join them.

"Let's go eavesdrop!" Leo says.

Before I can stop him, he's run across the yard and flattened himself against a tree. I sigh. Does he really think no one can see him now? I glance around to make sure Mrs. Kelly isn't watching us, but she's gone back into the house.

"I know Connor's really excited that David will be in his class in the fall," Mr. Kelly is saying. "He has a few friends but hasn't really found a good friend yet."

"Dad!" Connor whines, reddening.

"Don't feel bad, Connor," David says, stepping away a bit from his mom. "I don't have any friends here at all, so it's not a big deal that you don't have a good one."

I'm not entirely sure I follow eight-year-old David's logic, but I get that he's trying to make Connor feel better. The two boys run off to play in the sprinkler and the grown-ups keep talking.

"My wife told me a bit about the situation with your husband being ill," Mr. Kelly says. "Please let us know if there's ever anything we can do. David's welcome to stay here anytime you want to go visit your husband at the clinic."

"Thank you," she says. "I may take you up on that in a few weeks. As for now, we're just getting used to the new house. It's been a big move for David, a lot to adjust to at once."

"How did you choose Willow Falls? It's not very close to anything."

"There were definitely towns closer to Phil's clinic," she says, "but his side of the family has roots here. His great-grandfather was one of the first settlers, even before Willow Falls was a real town. They didn't live here very long, perhaps a decade or so before moving out west. Phil had always hoped to bring his family back one day." Her voice cracks on the last few words and Mr. Kelly puts his hand on her arm to comfort her.

"I'm sure he's happy that you and David are here now," he says.

She nods but doesn't try to say anything else. Mrs. Kelly comes out with piles of paper plates and napkins, and calls out, "Everyone find a seat for pizza!"

I pull Leo away from the tree and around to the side of the house, where there's a thick row of large bushes. "We really should stay out of the way until it's cake time," I remind him. "Then if we can't find a better way to stop Connor, we'll just have to tackle him and run." Not our best plan, but at least it's bound to work.

He nods and I ask him, "Did you know that stuff about David's dad?"

"Not all of it. If it's so hard for him to talk about it now, imagine what it must have been like when he was this age."

"I've been thinking about it. If we're in the past now, then that means the past still exists, like it never really went away."

He thinks for a minute. "I know what you mean. If the past is still here, do you think the future is here, too?"

"I don't know, maybe. I'd rather believe we make our own futures depending on what we do in the present. Even though right now for us the past IS the present and the present is the future and —"

Leo smiles. "Now you're getting too deep for me. Let's go where we can see the yard better."

We move a little closer and position ourselves at an angle where someone would have to be looking directly at us to spot us through the branches. It's fun watching David and Connor joking around and eating pizza like old friends instead of brand-new ones. Soon lunch is being cleared and the little kids are up and running again. "It's almost time," Leo says. "We need to get closer again, but they're gonna see us."

"I have an idea. We can tell them that when we were delivering the pizza, I dropped a bracelet or my phone in the grass and is it okay if we look for it?"

"Works for me."

"Which, bracelet or phone?"

He shrugs. "Whatever comes out of your mouth when you get there."

"Me? Can't you do it? You're a better liar than I am."

"That's not really a compliment, but fine." He stands up and gestures for me to follow. "Come on, Amy, let's go get that third check mark and free Grace."

"You got it, Leon." We high-five and I follow him out onto the lawn, pretending like I'm searching the grass. We don't get too far before Connor's grandfather appears before us. "Can I help you find something, young lady?" he asks in his rolling Irish accent.

Leo and I both instinctively duck our heads. The only time we've spoken to him was outside Mr. McAllister's Magic Castle Birthday Party Palace. He was nice enough, but I don't want to make a habit of it.

I force myself to look up so I'm not being rude. He's wearing the same hat that the bunny will chomp two years from now. "I, um, lost my bracelet," I say at the same moment Leo decides to say, "She lost her phone."

He looks from one of us to the other. "Which is it?"

"I lost both my bracelet and my phone," I say, "when we were, um, delivering the pizza?"

"Right," Leo says. "So we'll just look around for them, if that's okay."

We try to step around him, but he moves into our path. "I believe I might have seen the items you're looking for," he says.

"You have?" I ask, not expecting that response.

He nods. Up close I can see he's sweating a little around his forehead. He must be hot in that hat.

"I believe I saw them on the counter in the powder room. Might you have left them there?"

"That means bathroom," Leo tells me.

"I know what it means! Honestly, we're in all the same classes!"

"Let me show you," Connor's grandfather says. He puts his hands on our backs and walks us toward the house. I can see to my right that the cake is being set out on the long table. A glance to the left finds Connor playing catch with David.

"We can check it out later, after the party ends," Leo says. "We don't want to be in the way."

"It's no trouble," he says, pushing open the sliding glass door that leads inside. We pass through the kitchen until we reach a small bathroom off the living room. "I'd look around in there," he says.

We dutifully step inside.

"Thieves!" he shouts. "I saw you lurking in the bushes!"

We are both too shocked to reply. I open my mouth to speak, but he slams the door in our faces. Then before we can even think to move, he locks it behind him.

Chapter Seventeen

What kind of bathroom has a lock on the outside? We've tried pounding on the door, yanking the doorknob off, and are now trying to break the small window above the toilet. Leo has his hand wrapped up in a towel. I stand back while he punches the glass.

"OW!!!" He clutches his hand.

"Are you okay?"

He unwraps the towel and slowly flexes his fingers. "I guess nothing's broken. That looks a lot easier in the movies."

"Can you see what's going on out there?"

He nods and holds his hand out to help me up. We both squeeze onto the top of the toilet seat and are just in time to see David throw a Nerf football to Connor. Five seconds later Connor's shoulder is in the cake.

"Well, I guess we know how it happened now," I say, unable to keep the defeated tone out of my voice.

We climb down. I lean against the counter to sulk, and Leo sits on the toilet. If there were a mirror in here, at least we could distract ourselves by checking out our current appearance. Who doesn't hang a mirror in a bathroom? To lighten the mood, I say, "Hey, as far as we know, we could be circus folk. Like maybe I'm the bearded lady and you're the tattooed man."

"Could be," Leo says. "It would explain that dude's instant distrust of us." He springs up and yanks on the doorknob again. "Okay. This is how I see it. For some reason, Connor and Grace's grandfather thinks we're trying to rob the place and will probably have the police here after the party's over." He checks his watch. "Which is ten minutes from now. Getting arrested would not be cool, but I'm more worried about our bodies being torn apart as we're pulled forward in time from the wrong spot. We've always left the past a lot closer to where we entered it."

He's right. I shiver. Being torn into pieces is not at the top of my goals list.

But he's not done. "Also, what happens after we reappear in our own time? What if someone is using this very bathroom? They would have a complete heart attack!"

"Oh, no! You're totally right! It could be a parent or one of the doctors or anybody!" I pound on the door and shout, but everyone is still outside and the music is too loud, and all it does is hurt my knuckles. "I wish we could call Future Connor and give him a good reason why no one should use their downstairs bathroom." I pull out my phone but of course it says, NO CELLULAR SERVICE. This phone was only registered two years ago, and my phone number didn't exist yet. I hold it up to show Leo the message. "It's not like I could really call into the future anyway."

"But wait," he says. "Just because the phone doesn't work, the Internet still might!" He takes my phone and checks the settings. Sure enough, KELLYRED pops right up on the list of wireless networks. "Too bad we can't send an email five years into the future!"

"We can!"

Leo looks skeptical. "How?"

"Kylie did this project for school last year where she had to write a list of goals and then send them in an email to her future self! She only had to send hers a few months ahead, but it worked."

"How did she do it?"

"I don't know," I admit. "Do a search for how to send email to the future."

He still looks skeptical, but types it in. "Hey, there's actually a whole bunch of them!" He clicks on the first link and the page opens. "Tara or Rory?"

I give him a look.

"Right, Tara." He passes me the phone. "You're a faster typer."

I fill in Tara's email address and then write, *Tara, it's Amanda from the past. Long story, but we're locked in the bathroom by the kitchen in Connor's house. Please call him with some excuse about why he has to make sure no one uses the bathroom by the kitchen. Tell him Leo clogged it up or something.*

"Gee, thanks," he says, reading over my shoulder.

I schedule delivery for right after the party started, giving her time to spare in case she can't find him right away. I hit SEND and say a little prayer to the Internet gods that this website is still working in five years and that it gets sent out.

"Now we just have to hope we don't get arrested first!" Leo says with a grimace. He climbs back up to stare out the window.

I can't help it, I start to giggle.

"What's funny?" he asks without turning around.

"This whole thing. We're locked in a *bathroom* by an old man who thinks, what, that we're going to steal a five-year-old's birthday presents? In a few short minutes we'll either be arrested, stuck five years in the past, ripped to pieces, or, option number four, wind up sitting on some unsuspecting person's lap while they go to the bathroom. We're going to need a vacation from our summer vacation!"

He chuckles, but says, "I'll laugh about it when you're home safe."

"What about when *you're* home safe?"

He pauses before answering. "I care more about what happens to you."

I don't know what to say. So I clear my throat. "Is Mrs. Kelly still trying to put the cake back together?"

He peers back out the window. "Yup. Connor just got sent to his room. That means less than a minute to go."

I pull on the back of his shirt. "You should come down. We should stand as close as possible to the door in case option four happens. You don't want to be standing on anyone's lap! Or in the toilet if no one's on it and someone left the seat up!"

He scrambles off and we huddle together by the door. "Look on the bright side," I whisper. "Only a few seconds left, which means we didn't get arrested."

"True. And this room is much too small for a trampoline." He starts counting down the seconds. "Three . . . *please let Tara have gotten our email. . . . Two . . . I promise to be a better person and clean my room the first time Mom asks. . . . One!"*

White. Everywhere white. "Leo?" I call out, pawing my way through soft white air. Pieces of the air come off in my hand and stick to my face. "What's going on? Are we in heaven? Is this a cloud?"

"I'm here, Amanda!" he shouts, flailing his arms. The feathery strands begin to fall to the ground and I finally figure out what they are. The soft white air is actually toilet paper hung from the ceiling. From every square *inch* of the ceiling. I can't even see the door.

"Very funny, guys!" I call out, too relieved to be too annoyed. "Are you gonna blame this one on Ray, too?"

Rory and Tara burst into the bathroom, nearly knocking us over. They can only shake their heads because they're laughing too hard. Leo starts draping the long strands of toilet paper on their shoulders until they're nearly as covered with it as we are. It takes them that long to recover.

I sigh. "So I'm assuming you got my email?"

"Yes!" Rory says. "We ran over here as soon as it came through on Tara's phone. I'm sure Connor's parents thought there was something seriously wrong with us when we locked ourselves in the bathroom."

"There *is* something seriously wrong with you," Leo says, gesturing to the mess all around us.

"Hey, you're lucky Rory talked me out of the first idea," Tara says. "Water balloons."

"We've already been soaked once today with a surprise sprinkler attack. Where's Connor?"

"He's keeping guard by the kitchen door," Rory says. "He thinks Leo ate a bad burrito for lunch and is telling everyone to stay far away."

I nod approvingly. "Nice."

Leo groans.

We spend the next five minutes stuffing the last pieces of toilet paper into a big garbage bag and planning our next move. "The next party is the hardest one so far," I tell them. "It's about an hour away from Willow Falls at a relative's house. Connor sits down on top of one of the birthday gifts. The one Angelina enchanted, of course. Crushes it to bits. We're going to need Ray to drive us again."

"And an excuse to be in a stranger's living room," Leo adds. "We had today's party totally under control. We should be upstairs celebrating with Grace right now."

Rory checks her watch. "Bucky should be back from his trip by now. Let's go over there and see if he knows where Angelina is. If there's something she's not telling us, maybe he can. No offense, but you're kinda running out of days."

Since the Kellys live so close to town, it takes only a few minutes until we get to the community center. And then only a few seconds to find Bucky, due to the fact that he's currently onstage, playing his violin for the usual bridge and poker crowd that hangs out here in the middle of the day. A yoga class just got out and a few of the women are watching, too. Judging by his lopsided grin, Bucky is thoroughly enjoying the attention.

When he's done playing, we wait for his adoring fans to clear before we join him.

"How nice of you kids to visit on this fine summer day," he says, slipping his violin into a case.

"Hey," Tara says, pointing to the case. "Did you have to buy that? Did I forget to give you your blanket back? I'm really sorry. Things got kind of crazy after the play ended. I can get it back for you, or pay you for the case, or —"

He pats his new case lovingly. "No need to worry, dear. An anonymous benefactor had it delivered right here to the community center. The ladies can't help falling in love with me once they hear me play. Happens all the time." He winks.

Tara holds up the red envelope. "Speaking of ladies and love. Spill."

He squints at it, then shakes his head. "Never saw that before in my life."

"Bucky Whitehead!" Tara says.

"Oh, fine. What do you want to know?"

Leo nudges him in the arm. "So, you and Angelina, eh?"

"Leo!" the three of us girls say.

"What?" Leo asks innocently. "No use pretending we didn't read it."

Bucky sighs. "So we're having *this* conversation."

"We really don't mean to be nosy," I promise him. "We're just hoping you can help us with something."

"Come on, then," he says, leading us over to his favorite couch. He settles into his usual seat and we pull up chairs around him. "You know, my memory works a lot better with a full belly." He points to the desk at the front, which is currently set up for tea time. "All that playin' works up an appetite."

Rory jumps up. "I'm on it."

We wait for him to start talking, but he just hums along to the background music the community center pipes into the main room. I try not to show my frustration. Leo is not trying quite as hard. I have to kick him until he stops tugging at the loose threads on his armchair. The thing already looks like its best days were decades ago.

Rory returns and hands Bucky a plate piled high with crustless cream cheese and cucumber sandwiches. "Hope this is all right."

"Just fine, thank you." He rests the plate on his lap. "A drink would be nice, too."

Rory turns back around without a word. We watch as Bucky happily chomps on the sandwiches. Leo starts tapping his foot, which is at least less destructive to private property. Rory returns with a pink plastic cup of tea. There's nowhere to put it, so she winds up holding it awkwardly on her knee.

"So what can I help you with?" Bucky finally asks.

Tara hands him the card. "I found this last week near Angelina's seat at the bar mitzvah. It's the one I bought for you at the drugstore, so we know you sent it. Sorry we read it."

"We weren't planning to," Rory adds. "We thought maybe it would help us figure out where Angelina is. Somehow I don't think she's really gone fishing."

"Oh, but she has," he says, reaching for a sip of the tea. He hands it back to Rory. "A family reunion upstate. Lake, fishing, canoeing, the works."

Somehow I can't picture Angelina in a canoe! "And she'll be gone all week?" I ask, my hopes deflating.

"That's the plan," he says. "But you know the saying, 'Man

plans, God laughs.' That'll no doubt make more sense to you when you're older and have seen how life works out much different than you expect." He looks off into the distance and it takes Rory offering him some more tea to bring his focus back to us.

"I hope this isn't too personal, Bucky," I say, "but we really have a lot of questions for Angelina. Judging from your card, it seems, well, have you known her a long time?" I ask.

"You could say that." He leans back and takes a sip of tea. "Angelina was my babysitter."

Chapter Eighteen

"*Your babysitter?*" *we shriek.*

"Oh, yes, indeed she was," Bucky says calmly. "Although in truth I didn't need a sitter. Angelina was only a month older than me. My parents didn't think a boy with free run of the farmhouse could be trusted without female supervision." He chuckles. "I'd have probably gotten in less trouble on my own!"

I have to shake my head to clear it of the impossible image of Bucky and Angelina as children. "How come you never mentioned this before? All the times you told us about your childhood?"

He shrugs. "Those days are ancient history."

"But you obviously still care about her," Tara says. "You sent her this birthday card."

He wipes some crumbs off his lap. "Relationships are complicated."

At the same time we all mutter, "Tell me about it."

He chuckles. "Looks like I'm preaching to the choir on that one. Relationships are hard enough, but a relationship with Angelina is near impossible. She's ... how shall I put it ... *special.*"

We exchange looks. "How special would you say she is?" I ask cautiously.

When he doesn't reply right away, I add, "I mean, like, would you say she's able to do things that . . . um . . . other people can't?"

He lays down his last sandwich with only a bite left to go. "I might," he says after a short hesitation. "What are you getting at?"

There's so much to ask about, where do we even start? We'd decided on the way over that we weren't going to give away any of Angelina's secrets — at least the few of them that we know. "Well, she has a thing about birthdays. . . ." Tara says.

"Yeah," Leo chimes in. "What's up with that?"

Bucky looks down at his sandwich, and I'm afraid he's going to start eating again and ignore the question. But instead he says, "You're going to have to ask her yourself."

"We would," I reply, "but, like you said, she's on vacation. And this is kind of urgent."

"It's about Grace," Tara blurts out. "Grace Kelly."

He perks up. "The movie star?"

"Huh?" Tara says.

"Grace Kelly was a famous movie actress in her day," Bucky says, smiling at the memory. "Quite the lovely lady."

"This is a different Grace," Tara says. "She's only ten."

"Oh," he says. "Don't know her, then."

"She was in *Fiddler* with us last week. Red hair? Big personality? Short?"

"Not so short anymore, actually," Leo says under his breath.

Bucky taps his chin, deep in thought. "Oh, yes, I remember her. Cute kid. What does she have to do with Angelina?"

"Well . . ." Tara begins, clearly not sure how much she should reveal. She looks over at me. "Amanda?"

"It's like this," I begin, not really sure what's going to come out of my mouth. "Angelina's trying to help Grace, who went into this weird comalike state on her tenth birthday. And we're not sure if she's sick, like, physically or mentally, but it's pretty bad. And then we found out that Angelina and Grace have the same birthday and since, well, you know Angelina and the birthday thing, and —"

"I'm sorry, sweetheart," Bucky says, "but is there a question in there somewhere? I'm old. I might not make it to the end."

"Sorry!"

Rory pats my knee encouragingly.

I try again. "Okay, since you know her so well, here's a question, then. Is there anything you could tell us that might help us figure out a way to heal Grace? Like, maybe Angelina didn't tell us the whole picture?"

"When did Angelina ever give anyone the whole picture?" he asks. "She has her own reasons for doing things. You'd need a time machine to go back a long ways to understand her."

I don't dare look at Leo right now. He and I *are* a sort of time machine. I can't very well tell Bucky that, though. I lean forward. "Do you think there's a connection between their birthdays? Or is it just a coincidence?" As soon as I say the word, I want to bite it back.

"Come now, Miss Ellerby. You know there are no coincidences

in Willow Falls, especially not if Angelina is involved, as you say she is."

"I know, I know."

"And a tenth birthday, well, that's something special. It's a doorway between one world and the next. Between your past and your future. Childhood and what comes beyond."

"Now you sound like Angelina," Tara teases.

"I wonder what Angelina's tenth birthday was like," Leo says.

Bucky chuckles. "As I recall, she told her little brother she'd turn him into a turtle if he didn't do her chores for her. Now, I'm not saying she did it, but that boy was always a little slow after that."

"Sounds like Angelina," Rory says. "When exactly was that? Like, how old is she?"

He laughs. "I know better than to reveal a woman's age."

"Then how old are *you*?" Leo asks.

Bucky shakes his head. "Old enough not to fall for that. Let's just say we've both seen a lot of birthdays. Back then people didn't celebrate birthdays the way they do now. The only one of Angelina's that stood out was her eighteenth." His smile slowly fades as his face clouds over. "That was the last time I saw her truly happy and carefree. So beautiful — glowing, really, and ready to face the world head-on. Dancing with the gas lamps flickering all around her, the moon high above. Oh, what a night that was!"

When he drifts off into silence, I ask, "But what happened?"

He shrugs. "Things change. People change. You make some choices you can never take back." He stands up abruptly, not even noticing that he's knocked his empty sandwich plate to the floor. "The future is all possibilities, but the past is set in stone. All those ghosts of ourselves, our youth, still alive inside us, but out of our reach forever. We meet them when we close our eyes, when we let our memories come alive." He shakes his head. "But that's all they are. Memories. No more real than a dream."

Before we can ask him what he means, he drags a nearby folding chair up to one of the card tables and says, "Deal me in." We take that as our signal to leave.

Outside, we lean against the wall of the community center. We don't know much more than when we went in. Not anything that's going to help us with Grace, at least. The skies have clouded over, and the thick gray air suits our mood. I go over Bucky's parting words in my head until an idea starts to form. I push myself off the wall and face the others.

"Hey, what Bucky said in there, about the ghosts of ourselves still living? I think he's right. But not about the part where he said they're not real. We know that's not true. We *can* reach them, back in the past. Maybe not our own ghosts, but the ones inside other people. Angelina told us she tweaked the curse so we can keep going back to July fourteenth of different years, right? Maybe those years don't have to be the ones she listed in her notebook. Maybe it can be July fourteenth of *any* year. Including Angelina's eighteenth birthday!"

"Wouldn't she have told you if that was possible?" Tara asks. "Wait, never mind. Of course she wouldn't have."

"But how would you do it?" Rory asks. "We don't know where Angelina's party was, or even what year it was."

"Well, what did Bucky say?" I ask. "Dancing in the moonlight or something? With gas lamps?"

"It must have been a long time ago if there were gas lamps," Rory says.

"I bet it was Apple Grove," Tara says. "Didn't you guys say they used to have dances there?"

Yes! Where else could it be? I turn to Leo. "How long has it been since we've had a camping trip at the grove?"

"At least a year." He grins. "I'd say we're long overdue."

Chapter Nineteen

"**My mom wanted you to have these,**" Connor says, stepping out onto his porch. He hands us each a waffle wrapped in a napkin. Tara and I had ridden our bikes over to see if we could get any information on the best way to get into Grace's party today.

Tara tries to take a bite, then pulls it back out of her mouth. "I think it's still frozen."

"I know. My mom's kind of out of it. I don't think she's slept since Saturday."

It's now Friday morning. That's a long time.

I watch Tara trying to politely gnaw on her waffle. She was quiet on the way over here. Even though she doesn't say it, I know she's sad about not hearing from David very much.

"How's Leo's stomach?" Connor asks.

"What do you mean?" I ask between hard bites.

"He was stuck in our bathroom for, like, an hour yesterday? My mom said he went through three rolls of toilet paper! Must have been a pretty bad burrito!"

Tara giggles and I elbow her, although I'm having a hard time keeping a straight face, too. "He's fine now. Thanks for keeping everyone away. I'll let him know you asked."

"Where's the rest of your crew?"

I answer while Tara chews. "Rory's friend Annabelle dragged her to the mall, and Leo's helping his mom build some kind of compost heap in their backyard."

"My mom tried that once," Tara says, swallowing. "It's pretty much like putting a pile of garbage in your backyard. Good for the plants, bad for the nose."

"Maybe it would be good for the new trees at Apple Grove," I suggest.

"You heard what I said about the smell, right?"

"So how's Grace this morning?" I ask, changing the subject from garbage.

"Same," Connor says. "My grandparents flew in last night, so they'll be here soon to see her."

At the mention of his grandparents, the memory of his grandfather locking me and Leo in the bathroom pops into my head. I'm not so sure I want to see *him* again!

"Where do they live?" Tara asks.

"Down south. We only see them every few years."

I tilt my head at that. "Really? But doesn't your grandfather go to all your birthday parties? I mean, I thought I remembered Grace having a birthday party on the beach once when I was there with my friends. Old guy with really red hair?"

He shakes his head. "No, they don't come up here much. We usually go there."

"Oh," I say. "I must be confused, then."

"But I think I know who you mean. It's probably my great-uncle Bill. He's my mom's uncle." He scratches his head. "Or is it my dad's?"

"That must be the guy. He seemed . . . nice?"

Connor nods. "He never misses one of Grace's parties, and always helps out. He brings the coolest presents, too."

Okay, so now at least we know one guest who will be there today. Maybe there's some way to use that information to help us get in. I sure hope we will look different than we did at the backyard party. Although this one will have happened before that one, so he won't have actually *met* us yet. The rules of time travel, Angelina-style, are very confusing! But I think I have a plan.

.   .   .   .

"What's all this?" Leo asks as he climbs into Ray's backseat an hour later. "Did you rob a flower stand?"

"Never gonna get the smell outta my car," Ray grumbles.

I turn around in my seat. "Like 'em? They're part of my grand plan to get us into the party today."

He picks through the mound of roses, carnations, and lilies that takes up the other half of the backseat. "Do tell."

"I also have this!" I reach down and pick up a medium-sized cardboard box covered in yellow wrapping paper.

"You've been busy!"

"I've had help," I admit. "So basically here's the plan. I thought we could pretend to be delivering flowers from Grace's grandparents from down south, who won't be there. We know that Connor's other grandfather — who's actually his great-uncle Bill, by the way — *will* be there because Connor told me he never misses a party. We can wait till he arrives, then sort of walk in with him, like we belong. And the present is to switch out with the one that Connor sits on. I tried to match up the size with the one in the video. Pretty good plan, right?"

"Sure," he says. "But if we're delivering flowers, how come we need Great-uncle Bill? Wouldn't we just ring the bell and say we have flowers?"

I pause. "Yeah, all right. That's why you're usually the plan maker."

He reaches over and hands me a rose. "It's a good plan, Amanda. I think it will work."

We pull up to the house and Ray parks out front. "Hey," he says. "If you don't leave the car and the party starts, will you fall right onto the road?"

"Pretty sure we would," I say, thinking of our fall through the bench yesterday and my sore butt.

Leo brings the flowers and I have the box. We hide around the side of the house until it's time. The only way I can tell we're now in the past is that Ray's car is gone and there are two balloons tied to the mailbox. I peek around the corner in time to see Great-uncle Bill step out of his car. He looks a little younger than in previous years, not as stooped. He pats his hair into place, straightens his shirt, and reaches in for his gift. It's the same one I have in my lap.

"Great-uncle Bill just got here," I whisper to Leo. "And the gift that Connor breaks is *his*!"

Leo groans. "Great. Another run-in with crazy Great-uncle Bill. It felt like he locked us in that bathroom on purpose, ya know? Like he knew we were trying to keep Connor from falling into the cake."

"He couldn't have, though, right? I mean, he said he heard us talking and knew we were plotting something. Plus if he knew why we were really doing this, he'd WANT us to help Grace. Connor said he's a really good guy."

"I'm sure you're right," Leo says. "I'm just being paranoid. C'mon, let's get this over with." He thrusts the flowers at me and takes the gift. I wait until Great-uncle Bill has gone inside to ring the bell.

"Come in," a woman's voice calls out. "It's open!"

"That was easy," Leo mutters.

"She must think we're more guests." I slowly push the door open. "Flower delivery," I call out.

Heels clack on the wood floor and a pretty woman wearing a KISS THE COOK apron appears. She looks familiar from a few of the parties. "Oh, I'm sorry!" she says. "I thought you were my sister Ida. She's always late." I smile at her around the flowers.

"Oh my," she says, stepping back. "They really do make you get into costume, don't they?"

"What do you mean?"

"Unless you always dress like that," she says, laughing.

Leo grabs my shoulders and turns me toward a large mirror hanging in the hallway. I lower the flowers even more. We are both wearing cow costumes. COW COSTUMES. Our faces are colored with white paint. Black splotches dot our noses and cheeks. I have a TAIL. "I bet she's getting back at us for messing up the last one so badly," I mutter angrily.

"Moo," Leo replies.

"Here, let me take those," Aunt Millie offers. She reaches out for the flowers but I hold tight.

"Why don't we put them in water for you?" I ask. "It's sort of part of the job."

"Lovely! The kitchen is this way." She leads us down the hall. "You can lay them on the counter and I'll find some vases."

"They're, um, from Grace's grandparents," I tell her.

"Really?" Her brows rise in surprise, but she covers it up with a smile. "Hey, kids!" she calls out. "You must come see the flower-delivery people."

Connor and Grace and a bunch of cousins come running into the kitchen, sliding around in their socks. At four, Grace is even more adorable. She takes one look at us and her face begins to crumple. I'm afraid she's about to cry when Great-uncle Bill kneels beside her and says, "Wow! Will you look at them! Aren't those the best cow costumes you ever did see? They must be here to play birthday games with you, isn't that right?"

"Um, sure," I say, "we can sing a song for you."

"Moo," Leo adds, pushing the present behind his back.

"Let's all go into the living room so everyone can watch," Great-uncle Bill suggests. Grace reaches up for her uncle's hand, and Leo and I exchange a look. We hang back a step to let everyone file into the next room. "I'll keep their attention on me," I whisper, "and you switch out the present."

He nods and we move the box from behind my back to behind his.

"Wow," Mr. and Mrs. Kelly exclaim when they see us. "Great costumes."

Leo gives a little bow, careful not to reveal the box. "We're here to wish Grace a *moo-tiful* birthday!"

I cringe at his pun, but at least he's saying more than *moo*. I spot Great-uncle Bill's gift on the top of the pile on the coffee table. I can tell Leo sees it, too. I step into the front of the room so everyone's backs are to the pile. "Gather 'round," I tell the kids, waving my arms in big circles. I glance around in the vain hope that there might be a drum set that I can play, but of course there isn't. The only kids' song I remember is "The Wheels on the Bus," so that's what I sing. I do the motions along with it and hope my cow tail is swishing to the beat. Leo's right — I must be getting braver.

I watch out of the corner of my eye as he places our present next to the original, then lowers that one to the floor and slides it with his foot so it's behind the couch.

Everyone claps and asks for more. "I'm sure our lovely cow friends have to get to the next house," Mrs. Kelly says. "Plus we have gifts to open."

"We can stay through the gifts and sing more after," I offer.

"All right, then," Mrs. Kelly says, a bit hesitantly. She's not quite sure what to make of us. Grace claps her hands and Mr. Kelly starts piling the gifts on the floor in front of her. Our gift remains on the top. Great-uncle Bill reaches for it and turns it around. "Does anyone see a card in a yellow envelope?" His voice has an edge of panic to it not normally reserved for missing birthday cards.

I lean into Leo. "Did you notice a card with the other one? I didn't see it on the video."

"There could have been one taped to the back that we didn't see."

A few people join in the search while we try to blend into the wall, which is impossible due to our being COWS.

"Here it is, Uncle Bill!" Connor shouts, reaching behind the couch and lifting out the original gift. "That one must be someone else's!"

Leo and I cringe.

Great-uncle Bill takes the gift and pats Connor gratefully on the shoulder.

"Okay, Plan B," Leo whispers. "Stop Connor from sitting on it."

Everything unfolds so quickly after that. Grace begins opening her gifts with gusto. Wrapping paper flies everywhere. I wish there was a way to take back our fake one, but I can't think of anything.

To my horror, Mr. Kelly picks it up next and puts it in Grace's hands. She gleefully unwraps it and starts yanking at the box top.

"Do you even know what's in there?" Leo whispers, his voice edged in worry.

I shake my head. "Rory made it. It could be empty!" I can't bear to watch and squeeze my eyes shut.

"Wheeee!" Grace shouts. "It's Knuffle Bunny from the book!"

I allow myself to peek. She's swinging around a green stuffed bunny that looks awfully familiar.

"Isn't that Sawyer's favorite stuffed animal?" Leo whispers. "He's gonna freak when he can't find it."

I shake my head. "Rory told me once that her mom keeps duplicates around in case he ever lost it."

I give a silent prayer of thanks to Rory's mother for her forward thinking. And to Rory!

"Who gave Grace this lovely bunny?" Mrs. Kelly asks. When no one in the room lays claim to it, I slowly raise my hand/paw. "It came with the flowers."

Mrs. Kelly raises an eye. "How generous!"

Grace plops the bunny onto her lap and turns her attention to the next gift. Everyone else does, too, except for Great-uncle Bill. He is staring at us and then back at his own gift. I glance away, but can tell out of the corner of my eye that he is still staring. That can't be good. I watch him lean over Connor, who is sitting on the couch, and ask him something that I can't hear. Connor jumps up and runs into the kitchen. As soon as he's gone, Great-uncle Bill places the gift on the couch, right where Connor had been sitting, and lays a pillow gently in front of it. I grab Leo's arm.

"I saw it," he whispers anxiously. "We need to stop Connor from sitting back down."

Connor soon reappears, a glass of water in his hand. He heads back toward the couch and I lift my arm/paw to stop him. But before my hand reaches Connor's shoulder, Great-uncle Bill steps between us. He meets my eyes. "Please," he whispers. "Don't."

I don't think anyone has ever looked at me the way he's looking at me now. His deep brown eyes are literally begging. There is no more denying it. He knows something.

"But I'm trying to save her," I whisper. "Grace."

"So am I," he replies.

We stare at each other for what seems like an eternity. Up close like this he looks . . . off somehow. Like his features don't all match up.

Leo, unable to see Great-uncle Bill from where he's standing, nudges me. "C'mon, grab him."

But I can't turn away from those pleading eyes. My hand falls away. I watch as in slow motion, Connor places the water on the table, then plops right down onto the present, which shatters loudly. Everyone gasps and runs over.

"Thank you." Great-uncle Bill presses my hand before joining the others.

Leo is shaking his head in disbelief. "You had him. Why didn't you stop him?"

I drag Leo out of the room and share what happened on the way out the front door. "The way he looked at me! It was so intense. He really wanted Connor to sit on that present, maybe more than we wanted him not to. I don't know why, though." Instead of heading directly to the side of the house to wait to return to the present time, I lead Leo over to the car Great-uncle Bill arrived in.

"It's time for some real answers." I pull the door open and slide in. Leo climbs in the other side.

"What are we looking for?"

"Anything."

"There's a duffel bag back here," Leo says, reaching into the backseat. He unzips it to reveal a huge wad of cotton balls, a bottle of contact lens solution, a bag of bobby pins with strands of red hair sticking out of some of them, and a makeup kit with a business card tucked inside that reads, *Let Bettie Make You Beautiful.* Bettie is the makeup lady in town. She did the makeup for the play last week. Last he pulls out a well-worn brown wallet. "Should I open it?"

I nod and take a deep breath. Leo flips the wallet open to reveal Great-uncle Bill's driver's license. Only the man in the photo has white hair and blue eyes. And his name is Arbuckle Whitehead. We gasp.

It's *Bucky*!

Chapter Twenty

"*Wow, you look nice!*" *Leo says when he arrives* at my front door. He swings my backpack over his shoulder. "Should I go home and change?"

I shake my head. He's wearing tan cargo pants and a long-sleeved blue shirt. "You look fine. I just thought, you know, dancing in the moonlight and all, that I'd dress up a little." Kylie had lent me the sundress. When she'd asked why I wanted it, I told her I might be seeing a cute guy tonight. She tossed it to me without any more questions. Then she tossed me her lip gloss and hair straightener.

"Didn't your parents wonder why you're wearing a skirt to go camping?"

"They already left for their big Saturday night date." I yawn, unable to help it. After finding out that Bucky was the one trying to ruin Angelina's plans, I didn't sleep much last night. I don't think any of us did. He wasn't at the community center when we went to find him after returning from the party. We'd gone over it late into the night, trying to make some sort of sense out of what happened. At first Tara was convinced that Bucky must have been going back in time, too, but we were able to figure out that he couldn't have. He was in all the original videos. Plus Connor knew him even before all this. That means he must somehow have known how to stay one step ahead of Angelina, always ruining her plans and setting up Connor to take the fall. But why? He loves Angelina, and he seemed to honestly care about Grace, too. We're hoping that tonight gives us some answers.

Leo keeps looking over at me and smiling while we wait for Ray to pick us up. He steps a little closer and then pretends to "accidentally" drop his hand into mine. A movement out of the corner of my eye attracts my attention. I turn in time to see the curtain in Kylie's room move to the side. She stands framed in the window, watching. Before I can pull my hand away from Leo's, she lifts hers and gives me the thumbs-up. I turn back around before she can see me smile.

Ray pulls up in the SUV. Tara and Rory are already at Apple Grove. Leo tosses our backpacks into the backseat next to three rolled-up sleeping bags and enough snack food to last a week. I lift out a plastic container filled with a mixture of candy corn, M&M'S, and pink jelly beans. "My parents are trusting you to provide for our health and well-being. I don't think this is what they had in mind."

"Blame that on Emily," Ray says. "She wanted to come, but when she learned that Jake Harrison wasn't going to be there she changed her mind. Those snacks were supposed to be presents for Jake." He rolls his eyes. "I don't see what all you girls see in him."

"Me, neither," Leo says, climbing over the sleeping bags.

"Sure you don't," I reply, slipping into the front seat and helping myself to some of Emily's mixture. "Thank you for doing this, Ray. I'm sure you had better things to do with your Saturday night."

"Not really," he says, pulling away. "And I like sleeping under the stars. Reminds me of the outback."

"When you used to go camping all the time with the Rover Scouts?"

"Hey, don't dis on the Rovers. I learned some valuable skills from those mates. You can pitch your own tent, if you like."

"No, thanks," Leo says. "Go, Rovers!"

"That's more like it."

I munch on Emily's candy mix and try to focus on the job ahead. It was so hard missing Grace's third birthday party today, but between Angelina and Bucky, they've really left us no choice. It was at a petting zoo at one of the farms on the outskirts of town. Angelina had tried enchanting Grace's party hat, but somehow the string got cut and the hat wouldn't stay on Grace's head.

"Wake up, sleepyhead," Leo says, shaking my shoulder. I slowly open my eyes, disoriented. For a split second, the combination of Leo's arm fluttering back and forth and the dusky sunlight behind him reminds me of the SpongeBob SquarePants's balloon. I instinctively pull away and then yelp as the seat belt digs into my stomach. I sit up and wipe my mouth, hoping I didn't drool. It feels like I've been asleep a lot longer than the fifteen-minute drive to Apple Grove. "What time is it?"

"We let you sleep while Ray set up the tents. They're very sturdy. The other Rover Scouts would have been proud. Come see."

I smooth down my rumpled dress and follow him out into the clearing. Ray is busy taking a nap on his sleeping bag, and Rory and Tara wave us over to the campsite they've set up. I really *did* sleep a long time! The tents encircle a small fire pit, with a lantern at one end and the broken old fountain at the other. David's voice is streaming out of Tara's iPod. I always thought his voice sounded best right here.

Apple Grove at dusk is my favorite place in the world. The leaves from the big oaks splinter the sunlight into prisms and the air smells like wet earth, the kind that feeds baby apple trees. Our tiny trees may never bear fruit, but they'll be big and strong, and we'll string lights in their branches one day. The smell of apples hits me strongly, much stronger than usual. I turn to Leo. "Do you smell it?"

He nods. "We all do. I think it's a sign that we're on the right path."

"I hope you're right. But how do we know we won't wind up at someone else's birthday party? Think of all the parties that must have been held here on July fourteenth for the past hundred years, and we still don't know what year we need."

Leo smiles. "It doesn't matter what else happened here or what year Angelina's party was. We know all we need to know."

"We do? How?"

"Ask Rory," he says. "She's had a busy afternoon."

At the sound of her name, Rory looks up from impaling a marshmallow with a stick. I sit on a log beside her and she hands me the stick. Wiping her hands on her shorts, she says, "So get *this*. I went with my mom to pick up Sawyer at this camp he goes to at the community center, figuring maybe I'd catch Bucky there. I didn't find Bucky, but remember my friend Sasha, who takes those ballet classes upstairs? She's Kira's older sister. You know Kira, the who kissed Jake during the play and then fainted?"

"Amanda might not have met Sasha," Tara says, joining us. "She didn't sell cookies with us that day when the rest of us met her."

I let my marshmallow hover over the fire. "Yeah, I'm glad to have missed that one. Although I heard the uniforms were really something."

"I think I still have a wedgie from those shorts," Leo grumbles.

"Anyway," Rory says, "Sasha was there today, coming out of her dance practice. Sasha and Kira's family is related to Angelina somehow, like, really distantly, but they call her Auntie Angelina. So I said, 'I thought you were all up at the lake,' and she says, 'That's not till next week.'"

My marshmallow drops into the fire, but I barely notice. "So where is she, then? Did you find out?"

Rory shakes her head. "But I found out something else. Sasha asked me what I was up to this weekend, so I told her we were camping here, and without even asking, she said, 'Auntie Angelina talks about that place. People used to have parties there before the mall went up. Auntie says none of them could equal her eighteenth birthday, though. It was the first one ever held there.'"

"She didn't happen to say when it was, did she?"

Rory shakes her head again. "I asked, but all she said was that Angelina never reveals her age."

"It doesn't matter, though," Leo says, reaching into his pocket. "We know enough now." He pulls out Angelina's notebook and flips it open to the first page after Angelina's handwriting. I see he's already written down what Rory told us. How long was I sleeping?

I stand up and grab a bottle of water out of the cooler. "Okay, so we know it was the first party ever held here." I start pacing in circles around the campfire. "But we don't know what time the party started or where to stand in order to be sucked into the past. We could be in the totally wrong place at the wrong time."

"Or the totally *right* place at the *right* time," Leo says, grinning.

"Why are you smil — oh!" And just like that, we're in the middle of the biggest party I've ever been to. Instead of David's voice coming from Tara's iPod, an orchestra is playing a waltz. The air smells clean and fresh and strongly of apples, so much more so than in our time. No car exhaust from the mall parking lot. No mall at all! I guess we were in the right place after all!

I turn around to take it all in. The trees! Their full branches spread low and wide, forming a natural canopy above the dancers. Gas lamps sway in the branches, glowing although it is not yet sunset. The apples are full and ripe, even though it is still early summer. I can't take my eyes off them. "Leo, do you think the apple seeds Angelina gave us on our fifth birthday came from one of these trees?"

He's staring up at them, too. "I don't know. I think those were on our great-great-grandfathers' property."

"But Angelina told us Apple Grove *was* their property. Didn't she?"

Leo holds out his hand. "Let's skip the history lesson till later. Would you care to dance, Miss Ellerby?"

"Sure, why not." I take his hand and we join the couples swirling on the dance floor. A dance floor in the middle of the woods! Really it's a huge plank of wood, but still. Someone really went all out.

"Pardon us," a dancing boy in a top hat says, stepping neatly around me. His partner waves a white-gloved hand as the boy twirls her away, her long dress skimming the dance floor. Everyone is dressed a lot more old-fashioned than I would have guessed. I knew Angelina was old, but I didn't think she was *this* old!

Leo reaches for the water bottle that I'm still gripping and slips it in a pocket of his cargo pants. "Best to keep this out of sight. Judging by the clothes these people are wearing, I'm pretty sure plastic wasn't even invented yet."

I lean in for the dance. He puts his hands on my waist and I put mine on his upper arms. I murmur in his ear, "I hope whatever we look like now that we're dressed well enough."

"No one is pointing at us and laughing," he says, "so we must be okay. Unless they're just being polite and we're really farm kids dressed in overalls."

"Well, safe to say we're not cows anymore."

I let him lead me across the dance floor, doing my best not to trip or bump into any of the couples twirling around us. We reach the end of the dance floor and find ourselves in front of the old fountain. Except now it's shiny, new, and bubbling with water. It's the first familiar thing I've seen and is more proof that we're really here, maybe a hundred or more years in the past. For sure no one we know is even born yet. There are no cell phones, no email, no airplanes overhead. I shiver in the warm air, and pull closer to Leo. "Don't worry," he whispers. "We'll be okay."

I nod, trying to remember what my mom does when she gets anxious before a big job. *Breathe in through the nose, out through the mouth.* I do this a few times until I feel brave enough to suggest we explore.

Leo takes my hand and leads me off the dance floor. There are more people here than I'd originally thought. All ages, too, and not all of them are dressed as fine as the couples on the dance floor. There really *are* farmers in overalls, and they're chatting it up with businessmen in three-piece suits. Kids of all ages run around chasing one another and stealing cookies from the centers of the tables. All of the women are in skirts, and most wear bonnets or carry parasols. Everyone's feet are muddy since other than the dance floor, we are walking on the bare earth.

A waiter in a white tuxedo walks by with a tray of oysters. He holds it out to us. I can tell Leo is tempted, but we both politely decline. The aroma of simmering meat mixes with the sweet smell of apples and my stomach growls.

"This is so fancy!" Leo whispers. "I can't picture Angelina wanting this."

"Mother!" a young woman screeches behind us. "Please tell Amanda and Leonard they must go home now! They are RUINING my party!"

Chapter Twenty-One

Leo and I freeze. Angelina sees us! She knows us! And she must be really angry if she's using Leo's full name. I wish we could instantly disappear back into the present but it just doesn't work that way. We slowly turn around, ready to face Angelina's wrath. The young version looks almost nothing like the old one. Eighteen-year-old Angelina is fashionably dressed in a long skirt and a tight blouse, her dark hair in one long braid. In her heels she stands taller than I've ever seen her. I push through the fear and say, "We're so sorry, we didn't mean —"

But Angelina is not looking at us. She's watching two kids, no older than eight, shoving each other by the fountain. Angelina's mother, an attractive woman with hair piled high beneath a light blue bonnet, hurries over to split them up. "Leonard Fitzpatrick!" she scolds, pulling the boy aside. "I know your mama taught you better than to fight with a girl."

Leo and I gasp and grab on to each other for support. The red-faced boy has a head full of black curls and the girl has wavy blond hair, half of which is coming out of the pins used to keep it off her face. I can't take my eyes off them. It's like looking in that warped mirror again, from Grace's party at Mr. McAllister's.

The boy (Leo's great-great-grandfather???) points into the crowd. "She was standing up for that mean Rex Ellerby! I know he's here somewhere! Stop hiding Rex and stand up for your own self!"

The girl stomps her foot. "Rex is not mean! *You're* mean!"

Angelina's mother's lips twitch into a smile but she smothers it when Angelina taps her foot at her. "Children," her mother says in a calm, yet firm voice, "why don't you go back up to the main house and ask Cook for some ice cream. Everything looks brighter with ice cream in your belly."

A very handsome man in his midtwenties steps forward. He tips his tall white-brimmed hat at Angelina's mother. "I'll bring them up to the homestead," he says. "I was headed that way."

"Thank you, Mr. Smithy. And how are your plans coming to turn our little patch of land into a real town?"

"Very well, Mrs. D'Angelo. It's up to the county judge now, and then the state legislature will have to sign off, of course."

The boy Leonard stops glaring at little Amanda long enough to ask, "What will the new town be called, Mr. Smithy?"

"Well, I'm not quite certain yet, young Mr. Fitzpatrick. I am considering the name Willow Hills. Or perhaps Maple Falls. What would you suggest?"

Leonard puffs out his chest. "How about Fitzpatricktown?"

The crowd laughs.

He tries again. "Leonardville?"

"All right, all right," Mrs. D'Angelo says, pushing the boy toward Mr. Smithy. "We get the idea. Now go get that ice cream."

Leonard and Amanda run off into the woods, their fight seemingly forgotten. Mr. Smithy tips his hat before picking up a lantern and following them.

Leo (the one by my side) leads me over to a table, which has been laid out for a fancy meal. I grab on to the edge and lower myself into a chair. I realize I haven't taken a full breath since Angelina shouted our names. When I recover enough to speak, I finally notice that Leo has been uncharacteristically quiet. "Are you all right?" I ask him.

He nods his head, and when he does, a tear flies from his cheek.

"Are you crying?"

"Amanda, those kids . . ."

"I know."

"Without them, we wouldn't be here. We wouldn't be *us*. Their blood is in our veins. But they're just kids, like real people. Whenever I thought of them before, I pictured them in black-and-white, you know? Like those old photographs."

I nod. I knew exactly what he meant.

"Even the town founder, Mr. Smithy," he says. "Remember Angelina told us when we were eleven that Smithy was a quiet sort who only confided in his journal? But this guy doesn't seem like that. Maybe everyone is destined to be remembered wrong."

I hand him a cloth napkin from the table and he wipes his eyes. "I know it's all really hard to handle," I tell him, "but we have to shake it off. We don't know how long we'll be here and we need to find out why Bucky said everything changed after tonight."

Leo wipes at his face and takes a last look in the direction our great-great-grandparents went. "I know. But what if Bucky was leading us in the wrong direction? If he tried to ruin Angelina's plans all those years, maybe he's not on her side after all."

"But what about the card he wrote her?"

He sighs. "There's just so much we don't understand."

I lean back in my chair, resting my neck against the top. Even with the gas lamps on, the number of stars I can see takes my breath away. I point them out to Leo. "We're back before electricity. There's no way we'd be able to see this many stars otherwise."

"I think we're in the 1880s or early 1890s," he says. "I figured out once that our great-great-grandfathers' feud was somewhere around 1905. Angelina never told us they didn't get along even as kids!"

"Or that she *knew* them when they were kids!" I add.

Leo's face is suddenly very grave. "Amanda, we always knew Angelina was old, but she's REALLY OLD."

"I know."

He lowers his voice. "Do you think she found the fountain of youth or something?"

"If she did, you'd think she'd have made herself young forever, not old forever." I stand up and hold out my hand. "Come on, it's time to find out some secrets of the past."

"How?" he asks, letting me drag him along.

"The same way we learn secrets at home. By eavesdropping."

He grins. "Oh, right. Good idea."

We spot Angelina giggling with some girlfriends by the fountain, a glass of something bubbly in her hand. The girls are all swinging their parasols, which they no longer need in the absence of sunshine. I wish Tara and Rory could see this — they'd never believe it. Now that we're closer, I can see that Angelina is wearing heavy powder makeup. It does an excellent job of covering up her birthmark. I can only vaguely see the outline of the duck.

Now that it's fully dark with just the gas lamps to illuminate the night, it's easy enough to hide in the shadows of the trees. We pick one nearby and lean up against its trunk.

The girls begin to giggle. "When is he going to be here?" one of them asks.

"Any moment now," Angelina answers.

More giggling. "And you are certain he's going to ask you tonight?"

"He better! I'm not getting any younger."

Clearly Angelina doesn't yet know how very long her life is destined to be.

"Oh, here he comes!" one of them says. "The stars shine on you, Angelina D'Angelo. Arbuckle Whitehead is the most charming boy in the whole county."

"Come," says another, "we ought to give the lovebirds some privacy." With a last round of giggles, they run past us. Unable to help ourselves, Leo and I peek out from behind our tree.

"Wow!" I exclaim, unable to keep it in. "Move over, Jake Harrison! There's a new kid in town!"

Leo elbows me. "You're drooling over a man who's over a hundred years old!"

"Not from where I'm standing!" That whole "tall, dark, and handsome" thing is really working for Bucky. He's definitely movie star handsome. Not that they have movies yet. At least I don't think they do. I watch as he takes her hand and kisses the back of it. "You look beautiful tonight, Angelina."

"You clean up real nice, too, Bucky Whitehead."

"How you flatter," he says, smiling. "Shall we?"

"We shall." She lets him lead her to the center of the dance floor. The crowd makes room for them and then closes back up around them. I join Leo on the other side of our tree.

"So far, the night seems to be going great," I report.

"I give it another five minutes," Leo says.

But it happens in only two. A woman pushes her way through the crowd, shouting, "Where's the girl? I must find her!" I lean around the tree to look. She's dodging waiters and strolling violists, her eyes wild. The music is too loud for the dancers on the dance floor to hear her yet, but Mrs. D'Angelo does. She grabs hold of the woman's arm and pulls her aside. Leo and I inch farther around the tree so we aren't discovered.

"What troubles you, Sarah?" Mrs. D'Angelo asks. "Did the yarrow root not work for your toothache? Come over tomorrow for some clove if you —"

"My son Joshua is very ill! Please, you must help me." She tries to drag Angelina's mother away with her but has no luck.

"It is not I who can help you but my daughter. It is her birthright, not mine. Wait here, please. It's her birthday, as you can see."

The woman has no choice but to wait as Mrs. D'Angelo plunges into the crowd and pulls a red-faced Angelina off the dance floor. "Please, not now, Mama," she begs. "Not tonight. You promised me one last night of being a normal girl. Bucky just proposed, Mama. I said yes!" She holds her left hand out to her mother. Even from here I can see the small stone catching the light of the flickering lamps.

"You're *not* a normal girl," her mother replies in hushed tone. "I'm sorry, darling, I truly am. He's a lovely boy. He'll understand that this comes first." Angelina glances back at the dance floor. Bucky stands where she left him, watching, his hands pressed deep into his pockets.

When they reach her, Sarah grabs on to Angelina's arm as she had Mrs. D'Angelo's. "Please, you must come to the village. My son is only five. This morning he started feeling ill, and now at nightfall he is much worse. He complains of cramps in his legs and his feet. They have turned in. He cannot walk without falling."

Angelina's mother gives her daughter's cheek a gentle stroke, then steps away. Angelina looks pleadingly after her, but Mrs. D'Angelo doesn't turn around. Sarah continues her pleas for help. I can no longer hear their conversation, but Angelina holds up two fingers repeatedly. Sarah finally drops Angelina's arm and hurries back through the crowd, not meeting anyone's eyes. Without a second glance, Angelina runs back to Bucky and slips her arm through his.

He bends his head to hers. "Is everything all right, my darling?"

She tosses back her braid and nods. "Now that I'm with you."

I can tell without looking that Leo is rolling his eyes.

Waiters begin to flock to the tables with trays of hot food. Angelina and Bucky take their seat in the center, where they are joined by Angelina's girlfriends and a few other young men. None, I can't help notice, as handsome as Bucky.

"Look at her mom," Leo whispers.

I find Mrs. D'Angelo seated a few tables away. The guest beside her is chatting animatedly and pointing to the large red roses in the centerpiece, but Mrs. D'Angelo isn't paying her any attention. She's looking over at her daughter with the same disapproving look that all mothers give their daughters when they don't approve of their choices.

I guess some things never change.

Chapter Twenty-Two

While everyone eats, Leo and I sit under our tree. "Do you think what just happened with that woman is what Bucky was talking about?" I ask.

"Maybe. I'm not sure I followed it, though."

"Me, neither. But from what I could piece together, Angelina has some kind of responsibility to help people, but tonight she just wants to be a teenager. I think she was trying to tell the woman she'd come after the party, but I'm not sure."

"I don't know how any of this is helping us cure Grace," Leo says. "Maybe we're on a wild-goose chase here. Speaking of goose, do you think anyone would notice if we had some dinner? That food smells good!"

Keeping Leo from food is an impossible task. "Just lay low. More of our relatives might be lurking nearby."

That's apparently all the permission he needs. "I'll get you something, too," he calls over his shoulder.

I lean back against the tree trunk. Although ablaze with stars, the sky is quiet, too. No planes, no satellites in orbit, no space station. Just other stars and other planets. Right now, in this very spot, Tara and Ray and Rory are looking up at the same stars, though they can't guess how many are really out there, hidden by decades of light and pollution.

"Have you fallen, miss?" a deep voice asks from above. I look up, hoping to find Leo with a plate of food. Instead, a young man in a very high collar that looks uncomfortable in the heat, is kneeling beside me, concern in his eyes.

"I . . . I'm fine, thanks. I mean, thank you." I guess young ladies aren't supposed to sit on the grass and lean against trees at fancy parties.

He tilts his head at me. "Are you one of the D'Angelos' relatives from upstate? I cannot quite place your accent."

I glance around for Leo to rescue me, but don't see him. "Um, I live pretty far away, I mean, not far from Willow Falls in terms of miles, but still, um, far." I'm rambling, but I can't help it. I didn't expect to have to talk to anyone.

"Willow Falls?" he asks, scratching his head. "Is that the name Smithy landed upon? I thought he was championing for Willow *Hills*. Although now that I think on it, there are no hills here to speak of, now, are there?"

I stare at him, realizing what I said. "I . . . I'm just confused about the name." I wave my hand in front of my face. "It must be the heat. I feel a bit woozy."

"You must let me get you some water. I shall be right back." He strides off toward one of the tables before I can stop him.

"I leave for five minutes and you've found a new boyfriend?" I don't need to turn around to know that this time it's Leo. "Who said I have an old boyfriend to replace?"

He grins and kneels beside me. "A pretty girl like yourself? I'm sure the boys are all fighting over you." He places a large plate on my lap. The edge is rimmed with what looks like gold. It is quite beautiful. I can't say the same for the brown chunk of meat sliding around in what I think are mashed potatoes. "What is it?"

Leo already has his first piece in his mouth. "I think it's mutton," he replies between chews. "Or wild boar?"

"Mutton or wild boar? We're not in medieval times!"

He shrugs. "Probably steak, then. It's good. Aren't you gonna try it?"

I push the food around with my fork, wishing I'd thought to stuff my pockets with Emily's candy mixture. My new friend returns and hands me the water. "I apologize," he says, tipping his hat at Leo. "I did not know you were here with someone." He backs away, bowing as he goes.

"He was sweet," I say.

Leo grunts and spears my chunk of nameless meat with his fork. I lay my fork on my plate, not hungry anymore. I don't think we're going to figure out anything here. Maybe we shouldn't have let Bucky and what he did at the last party distract us. Maybe we should just finish what we started with Angelina and leave this all behind us.

I'm about to share my thoughts with Leo when he reaches for the glass of water my suitor had brought me, and brings it to his lips. I grab it back. "You shouldn't drink that. They don't have the same water-filtering processes that we have. Didn't you learn anything on all those school trips to the reservoir? There could be all sorts of things living in there. You'll thank me later when a tapeworm *doesn't* crawl out of your —"

"Hey!" he says. "I just thought of something! The two people we most want to speak to are right there." He points around the tree. "Not even thirty feet away!"

"Don't even think it, Leo Fitzpatrick! If you're worried about my plastic water bottle messing up the time line, imagine what confronting Bucky and Angelina would do!"

"I know, I know. Man, it's frustrating. I wish Bucky would just tell us what he meant about Angelina changing and why he was pretending to be related to Grace and Connor." He digs back into his food again, or rather *my* food. The tempo of the music changes to something much faster. At the same time, the chattering voices and the sounds of silverware clinking against bowls and plates abruptly cease.

"Why don't you ask him yourself?" I suggest.

"Huh? But you said we can't."

"Not young Bucky . . . old Bucky. Look. We're back!"

He looks up from his food and follows where I'm pointing. A familiar white-haired man ambles toward us, using a long walking stick for support. Gone are the gas lamps and almost all the stars. The lights from the mall parking lot are on, which makes it much brighter than it should be for this time of night. We scramble to our feet, holding the fancy plates, which apparently have made it through time with us. Looks like we're thieves after all!

Tara catches sight of us. "They're back!" she shouts, shutting off the music coming from her iPod. The others jump up from their places around the campfire and stop short when they see Bucky. We meet in the middle, by the fountain. It's jarring to see it crumbly and broken again.

We all start talking at once and no one can figure out what anyone's saying. Ray puts his fingers in his mouth and lets out a shrill whistle. "Respect your elders," he commands. "Mr. Whitehead, you go first."

"Please, ladies first," Bucky says, gesturing to me. He's still charming a hundred years later.

I have so many questions for him, I don't even know where to start. The easiest first, I guess. "What are you doing here?"

"Let's sit down, if you don't mind. We've got a lot to talk about and these bones are old."

Ray sets up a beach chair for him and Bucky sinks gratefully into it. The rest of us pull up logs around the fire. Tara shows Bucky the bags of snacks. "In case you need to eat first."

He holds up his hand. "I'm fine." To me and Leo he says, "I saw you disappear at the beach a few days ago."

I turn to Rory and Tara. "I thought you said no one saw us?"

"Hey," Tara says with a shrug, "we were busy dealing with a movie star in shock."

"Following you to the beach was just a test to see if my theory was right," Bucky says. "When Grace was rushed to the hospital last weekend, I knew Angelina would follow her there. And with Leonard and Rex's curse and your blackboards, well, I started putting the pieces together."

Leo and I share a surprised look. Leo asks, "You know about our great-great-grandfathers' curse? I mean, enchantment?"

Bucky nods. "I'm sorry I couldn't tell you anything sooner. Whatever my issues with Angelina, I respect the need to stay out of the way of one of her 'projects.' Everyone is on their own path, as she is so fond of pointing out."

"But you didn't stay out of the way this time," I say. "In fact, you seem very much in the way, *Great-uncle Bill*! You locked us in a bathroom!"

The lights in the mall parking lot switch off all at once, and in the firelight I can see all the lines crisscrossing Bucky's face. Now that I know how old he really is, it's amazing that he looks as good as he does. There is a weariness in his eyes, though, probably caused by a lifetime of holding in secrets.

"I promise to explain, but I need to start much earlier." He takes a deep breath and his words tumble out like a dam has been broken. "Angelina came into her powers at ten years of age. Her family had no idea how to help her. She described seeing things no one else could. Histories and secrets she could not have known. She could make things happen. It was overwhelming. Then a few weeks later, an old woman showed up on their doorstep who said that only she could help. She taught Angelina all she knew, with the understanding that when she turned eighteen, she would be expected to take over the woman's responsibilities. Angelina didn't know what those would be exactly, and mostly she did not want to know. She did not embrace these powers. In fact, she rebelled quite often. Her parents tried to keep word of their daughter's abilities quiet, but of course people found out. Still, they did their best to keep her happy and wanting for nothing. Her eighteenth birthday was to be a grand party, the last time Angelina could be a girl, carefree and surrounded by people who wanted nothing more from her than her company." He turns to me and Leo. With hope in his voice, he asks, "Did you see her? Did you get back there?"

With the sounds and smells from the party still fresh in my head, I tell everyone what we saw and what we heard. Tara and Rory keep interrupting to ask for more details about what Angelina looked like, or what she was wearing. I can't blame them for wanting to be able to picture her as a girl not much older than ourselves. Bucky blushes when I relay the conversation Angelina's friends were having about him being so handsome and charming. Well, maybe they only said charming, but I didn't want to tell them it was *me* who thought he was so good-looking. Ray says, "Way to go, mate!" and tries to high-five Bucky when I get to the part about the marriage proposal. Bucky's too busy twisting his hat in his hands to oblige. I finish by telling them about the woman, Sarah, rushing into the party.

"She was too late," Bucky says, staring into the fire.

"Too late for what?" I ask.

A faraway look settles into his eyes as he speaks. "Angelina went to see Sarah's little boy later that night, after the guests had all gone home. But she could not cure him. She used all the spells she knew, and even tried mixing herbs and applying salves as a last resort, but nothing could make the boy's muscles work anymore. He did not get worse, but he did not improve. Angelina blamed herself for not getting to him sooner, for not being strong enough to help him. After that, she kept to herself, studied, and turned down every invitation that came her way."

"Including yours," Tara says.

"Yes, including mine. She gave me my ring back, although I never stopped trying to get her to change her mind." He sits quiet for a moment, and we all inch forward, hanging on his every word.

"She spent the next year working ceaselessly to come up with a way to protect the children in the area of what would, by year's end, become the town of Willow Falls. She finally figured out the correct spell, or benediction, as she called it. As a penance, to make up for her selfishness, she was determined that every child born in town would be kept healthy. She insisted that she be called within the first hour of a child's birth, so that she could impart this benediction of hers. This became much easier in later years, when people began having babies in hospitals and she could just show up, without being invited. She never told anyone what she was doing; only myself and her parents ever knew. Her family is long gone now, of course. All these years later, she is still serving her penance. I have tried to tell her that her debt has been repaid, many, many times over again, but she cannot see it. Or will not."

"Why is Angelina able to do all this stuff?" Leo asks. "Her mother said it was a birthright? What's a birthright?"

"It usually means some rights you are born with," he explains, "like an inheritance. But in this case, Angelina wasn't born into a line of powerful women. Oh, her mother could mix a tincture to soothe an upset stomach or rid you of warts, but this was different. There is a vortex of power in this town, not far from this very spot, actually —"

"A vortex of power?" Leo repeats. "That sounds made up."

"I assure you, it is not."

Rory pinches Leo on the arm. "Ow!"

"Go on, Bucky," I urge. "What does this vortex do?"

"Mostly it just sits there, soaking up the energy of the world around it and funneling it back into the earth. But once every century or so, the power surges on one particular day. One baby born that day will have the ability to see the lines connecting us to one another, tethering us to our pasts, propelling us into our futures. Not only to see these lines — these streams of energy — but to control them, and to protect the people within their boundaries. Angelina was that baby." He takes a deep breath. "And as you've likely figured out by now, so is Grace."

Chapter Twenty-Three

We all stare across the fire at him, our mouths gaping open. Rory is the first one to find her voice. "If Grace can do all of that, why did she wind up in the hospital, not even able to move?"

I run Bucky's story back in my head and think of Grace and what's been happening to her all week and suddenly I know the answer. I jump up from my log. "Angelina did it! She put her in that frozen state!"

Bucky closes his eyes while the others turn to me, mouths open in surprise. "No way," Leo says. "Why would she do that only to send us back to fix it? That doesn't make sense."

I start walking in circles around the campfire. "I know it sounds crazy, but think about it. Angelina never tells anyone the whole story. She knew it was Grace's tenth birthday, and that she would come into her powers on that day. Maybe she wanted to keep Grace silent. To keep her from revealing all the town's secrets, and Angelina's secrets, in particular."

"That does sound like something Angelina would do," Rory admits.

"But then what were we doing at these parties?" Leo asks. "Each time we fixed one of them, Grace got a little better."

Tara shakes her head. "We spent a lot of time with her while you guys were in the past. Each time you came back with a check mark in your notebook, Grace changed, but I don't know if it was for the better."

"She grew four inches!" Leo argues. "She doesn't look so much like a stiff breeze could blow her away as she used to. That's definitely for the better, right?"

Bucky finally speaks up. "Grace's health *did* improve when Amanda and Leo unlocked the first two of the necessary three benedictions, that is true. But Angelina had altered the benediction she gave Grace — or tried to give her — on the day of her birth. It was not only intended to keep her healthy like the rest of the children in town, but it would block her from receiving her powers on her tenth birthday. Each time Amanda and Leo were successful in changing the past, Grace's body improved, but her powers dimmed. One more time and she would no longer have been able to access them at all."

"But why would Angelina want to keep Grace from getting her powers?" Tara asks.

Bucky continues. "Mostly she did it to protect Grace. She remembered what it was like for her all those years before and did not want to put Grace through that. Life was quieter back when Angelina was young. You could hide, and the whispers didn't travel too far. Today, if everyone knew that a young girl could see the past, weave the present, and change the future, well, you can imagine how quickly word would spread. She wanted Grace to have a normal life, one she herself was denied."

No one says anything as his words sink in. "But why did *you* get involved?" Leo finally asks. "You went to all of Grace's parties to make sure Angelina's plans failed, right? And did you use some kind of magic, too? To make yourself look so different?"

"It's true that I've learned a few tricks over the years — like the barrier that kept Angelina at a distance, and getting poor Connor to ruin the parties with little memory of it — but as for my disguise, I simply had a good makeup lady. That Bettie works wonders with a tub of cream and a tin of powder," Bucky says. "The red wig was my idea."

"But why would you do that if you loved her?" Rory asks. "Angelina, I mean."

Bucky rubs his hand across his face. At this point he looks every one of his years. But his voice is strong when he says, "That's exactly why I did it. I *did* love her. I still do. And believe it or not, I love Grace, too. So, yes, I made certain each year that Angelina's benediction didn't work. She never seemed to figure out I was behind it. It is time for her to let go of her guilt and move forward in her life. She deserves it. And the only way it will happen is if she lets Grace have her birthright."

He turns to me and Leo. "When Angelina realized on Grace's ninth birthday that she'd lost her last chance, she got you two involved. I couldn't figure out what she was planning, although I knew it would happen on Grace's tenth birthday. Angelina had tried returning to the past many times, the last being about thirty-five years ago, but she could never change it in the ways she wanted. I never thought she'd try again by sending the two of you. Clearly I was wrong. Unless you two were *not* disguised as cows at Grace's fourth birthday party?"

"Cows?" Tara and Rory shout.

I redden. "We may have left out that part of the story due to its embarrassing nature."

"Moo," Leo mumbles.

"I didn't know who you were at the time, of course," Bucky tells us. "We hadn't even met yet. All I knew was that my plan was about to be ruined. I had to step in and stop you. I didn't mean to deceive Connor or his family, and we have become close over the years. I know I will have to explain all this to them, a conversation I do not relish having. And I know it was taking a chance that Grace would get sick without Angelina's benediction, but outside of Willow Falls, every other child in the world faces those same risks every day. I had to weigh that against the fact that she would be robbed of what she had coming to her. We don't know why the vortex selects the people that it does, or anything else about it. But it's a gift, not a curse. Although Angelina doesn't always look at it that way, she has experienced great joy in helping people and has an understanding of the world that the rest of us never get. She can weave individual strands of energy and connect people to each other."

"Kind of like knitting?" I ask, thinking of the motions Grace had been making with her hands.

"Exactly," Bucky says.

"But wait," Leo says, "you weren't there during the magic show when Connor took the bunny at Grace's seventh birthday. If he hadn't taken it, Angelina's enchantment would have worked and you would have failed to stop it."

He chuckles. "That darn bunny. She ate right through my favorite hat. Those two kids I spoke to outside, that was you?"

We nod.

"You have to remember, from where I stood, you hadn't come back to the past yet. I'd fixed every birthday up to that point, so I figured I could risk letting one go. Always had a soft spot for bunnies. Figured Connor might, too."

Rory shudders. "You must never have had one for a pet."

Leo reaches into his back pocket and pulls out Angelina's small notebook. Seeing it reminds me that our job still isn't done. "Bucky, we still have two more of Grace's birthdays left. We skipped today's so we could go to Angelina's party. What happens if we don't go to the rest? Will Grace ever wake up?"

"Not on her own," he admits. "Only Angelina can undo it, and you know how stubborn she is. She's up at the lake house and who knows when she'll return."

"But she's not at the lake," Rory says. "We figured you knew that and just made up the story so we'd stop looking for her."

Bucky lowers the water he was about to sip. "She's not at the lake house? You know this for a fact?"

Rory nods. "So where is she?"

"I have no idea," Bucky says. His shoulders sag. He's clearly upset, but I'm not sure whether it's because he's worried about her, or because she went somewhere without telling him.

"It's very late," Ray says, picking up one of the lanterns. "I think we should call it a night. Bucky, I'll lead you out to your car. Are you going to be all right driving home?"

Bucky nods and pushes himself back up. "You're all good kids. I know you'll do what you think is right."

The three of us girls take turns giving Bucky hugs. He holds on extra tight when it's my turn. I think it's his way of saying he's sorry. Leo is busy scribbling in the notebook and waves good-bye instead. I recognize that look on his face. He gets very absorbed when he's working on a new poem. And after the week we've had, I'd be surprised if he doesn't get a hundred poems out of it.

"Look," Tara says as we head toward our tent. She points to the fountain. Max and Flo, the two hawks that we often see here when we're visiting the grove, have perched on top of it.

"Maybe they've come to protect us while we sleep," Rory says.

Tara smiles. "I think they've come for the fountain. They've been drinking out of it since my parents' eighth-grade dance."

Rory and I turn to her in surprise. "How do you know that?" Rory asks.

Tara shrugs. "Some things you just know."

I put my arm around Tara's shoulders. "Congratulations! You've mastered the art of the answer that's not really an answer. That makes you an official Willow Falls resident now!"

She laughs. "I guess I am."

We watch the hawks groom each other with their talons before they lean against each other and close their eyes. "So," Rory says, pulling the flap of the tent aside for me to go in, "what was that about you and Leo being cows?"

Chapter Twenty-Four

It's a tight fit with the three of us, but I'm having fun trading stories late into the night. We purposely don't talk about anything to do with Grace or Angelina or Bucky. Mostly we reassure Rory that it definitely isn't crazy that Jake likes her. Tara tells us that she thinks David was going to kiss her when he came over last week with her birthday present, but her uncle wouldn't leave and kind of ruined the moment. Then Rory says to Tara, "You ask her." And then Tara says, "No, you ask her." And they start hitting each other with their pillows so I say, "Yes." And they stop hitting each other and start hitting me.

"Why didn't you tell us?" Tara asks.

"I don't know." I push my face into my pillow so I don't have to meet their eyes. "It was just weird."

They sit up and crowd around my sleeping bag. "Leo's a weird kisser?" Tara asks.

"That's not what I said!"

"What, then?" Rory asks, trying to pull the pillow off me.

"It was . . . nice," I mumble into my pillow.

"Nice?" Rory repeats. "Your best friend for thirteen years, minus the one you weren't talking, finally kisses you and it was *nice*?"

I peek out from behind the pillow. "Okay, it was better than nice."

"Are you gonna do it again?" Tara asks.

Rory throws her pillow at Tara's head.

Tara tosses it back off. "What? It's a simple question!"

They sit still and wait for my answer. "I hope so!" I finally say and put the pillow back over my face.

They start hitting me again and laughing until Ray shouts that we're going to wake the bears out of hibernation even though it's July.

It feels like I've only just fallen asleep when the sun streaming through the thin walls of the tent wakes me. I try to turn over but Rory's feet are in my face. Plus I need to use the bathroom, otherwise known as the woods.

I unzip the tent flap as quietly as I can, grab my sneakers, and crawl out. The sky is still a mix of pink and yellow. A blue jay has replaced Max and Flo at the fountain, and Leo is sitting by the burned-out fire with Angelina's notebook in his hand again. His hair is all rumpled and he's still in his pajamas. I wish I'd thought to bring a hair band. Or had worn nicer pajamas instead of old sweats and my BORN TO ROCK T-shirt.

He waves me over. "The woods" will have to wait. "Hi," I say quietly so as not to wake anyone else. I sit on the opposite side of the fire pit so I don't assault him with morning breath. I tuck my hair behind my ears in a futile attempt to make it look neater.

"Hi," he replies with a smile.

"Hi, again."

"I like your T-shirt."

I look down. "This old thing? I got it on an adventure with

some guy a few years ago. Remind me to tell you about it some day. He got one, too, but he lost his."

Leo gets that mischievous glint in his eye and says, "So, I hear you'd like to kiss me again sometime?"

If I had a pillow, I'd throw it at him. "You heard us?"

"Your tent was all of two feet away."

I feel my cheeks growing hot. "Maybe I was talking about some other guy."

We hear rustling coming from my tent and thankfully Leo changes the subject. He opens the notebook to a page near the end and hands it to me. I'm surprised he's showing me his poem at this stage. Usually he doesn't like to show them to anyone until he's done a few drafts.

The last few pages are filled with his small handwriting. But I quickly realize he hasn't written a poem at all. Rather, it's a letter to Angelina! Skimming it, I can see he told her all about last night, and what we learned. It ends with a plea to free Grace. I look up at him questioningly.

"I thought since she can somehow make those check marks and Xs in there from wherever she is, maybe it would work both ways and she'd see it somehow."

"That's superbrilliant."

"She hasn't answered, though," he says, poking at the ashes with his old marshmallow stick.

I look up at the sky. The last traces of sunrise are almost gone, but it's still very early. "Maybe she just hasn't seen it yet." I flip back a few pages and see the familiar Xs and check marks — more Xs than checks. When I get to Grace's third birthday, the one we skipped to go to Angelina's party, a big question mark appears on the page. The paper is also sort of warped in spots, like it had gotten wet and dried that way. Almost like . . . almost like tears had fallen on it. I close the notebook and hand it back. I feel like I peeked at Angelina's diary.

Laughter comes from my tent and then Rory comes running out, wearing one shoe and holding up Tara's phone. "Look what Jake texted to Tara for me!"

"Seriously," I say, reaching out for it, "you've got to get a better phone."

"My parents said if I can go three months without losing my current one, they'll get me a real one."

"So basically you're stuck with your crappy one forever."

"Probably!"

I look down at Tara's phone and then burst out laughing. It's a picture of Jake puffing out his cheeks. He's wearing an eye patch over his left eye, and a ski hat pulled down over his right ear.

"He's pretending to be me from last year!" Rory says, beaming.

"I got that." I hand the phone back to her. "And to think you doubted how he felt about you!"

She grins and runs back into the tent. I turn back to Leo, hoping he'll go back to his tent so I can run into the woods. No such luck. He's standing by the fountain, holding the notebook open.

"Look," he says

I cross over to him and we peer into it together. The last page has five words written in red ink that definitely weren't there two minutes ago.

I'm still not strong enough.

I've never, EVER heard Angelina admit any weakness of any kind. "Do you think that's her response to your letter? Or something else?"

"I have no idea. Why wouldn't she be strong enough to undo whatever she did to Grace, if she made her this way in the first place?"

We stare down at the words, but they don't change and nothing else appears. Leo takes the notebook back to the tent he shared with Ray while I go in and tell the girls.

"It may not make sense," Tara says, "but at least she's communicating with you."

"She still hasn't heard from David," Rory explains.

"Oh." We roll up our sleeping bags and bring our stuff out front. I really don't feel like changing back into my dress from last night and hadn't thought to bring another change of clothes. Leo's stuff is piled outside his tent, too.

Tara turns in a circle. "Where's Ray?"

Leo points back to his tent. We sneak closer and are greeted by gentle snoring. That mischievous glint appears in Leo's eyes and he raises one eyebrow. I nod. He creeps over to the corner of the tent and starts lifting out the pegs. Rory and Tara run around to the back and do the same. In a few seconds, the tent has collapsed.

"Stone the crows!" Ray shouts, thrashing about and shouting more random Australian sayings. We burst out laughing and the thrashing stops. "Very funny," a muffled voice says.

Tara feels around for the zipper and undoes it. A rumpled Ray appears. He must have slept in his clothes because he's still wearing them. "It was Leo's idea," Tara says.

Ray runs his fingers through his hair, which somehow falls perfectly into place. He shakes his head at Leo. "I thought we were mates, dude."

"Sorry, couldn't pass the opportunity by."

Ten minutes later we're on the road. The atmosphere in the car is much different than on the way here. Everyone's lost in their own thoughts. Well, except for Ray, who has kept up a steady stream of ways he's planning to get back at Leo.

We pull up in front of Grace and Connor's house. We hadn't asked Ray to take us here, though I think we all knew this is where we'd wind up. It's still really early, but Tara texts Connor to let him know we're outside. A few minutes later, he appears at the door and beckons us in.

The house is quiet when we enter. We tiptoe upstairs behind him. Grace's door is open, and Mrs. Kelly is asleep on a cot set up in the corner. "This is usually where I find one of my parents in the morning," Connor whispers. We huddle in the doorway. "It's okay, you can come in."

Grace is tucked under the covers, her eyes wide open, her breathing ragged. Her coloring looks good, though, and Mrs. Kelly must have washed her hair because it's spread out on her pillow.

"We used to close her eyes at night," Connor explains, reaching across the nightstand for a bottle of eye drops. "But they just spring back open after a few minutes anyway." He leans over and, with a steady hand, squeezes a few drops into each eye. Grace doesn't blink when the soothing drops land. Instead, she bolts straight upright, smiles widely, and says, "But *I* am."

Then she falls right back to sleep.

Chapter Twenty-Five

Our jaws all fall open. "Did that just happen?" Connor asks, rubbing his eyes. "Or are we still dreaming?"

"That just happened," Rory says.

Connor reaches over and gently shakes Grace's arm. Grace mumbles something and slowly opens her eyes. They are bright and clear. "Hey, bro," she says in a crackly, hoarse voice. "How about some water?"

Connor shouts with glee, and Mrs. Kelly shoots up and flies across the room onto Grace's bed. Through her hugs and her sobs, she asks, "Are you okay? Can you sit up? Does anything hurt?"

Mr. Kelly runs in, wearing his pajamas, not even giving us a second glance. I guess he's seen stranger things this week than a group of kids in rumpled pj's. They all hug, they cry, they laugh. Mr. Kelly helps Grace sit up. She smiles at each of us in turn and then asks her mother to take out the IV tube. Mrs. Kelly hesitates for a second, then shuts off the valve and gently pulls it out of Grace's arm. Her father runs out of the room to call the doctor, while her mother runs downstairs to get some water and food.

We still don't know if Angelina is blocking Grace's powers or not. I take one of her hands in mine and Connor takes the other. She looks fully awake now. In fact her face is glowing. I think her expression of amazement is permanent, even though she's not stuck with it now. "Grace, what do you see?"

Connor looks up at me, surprised at my question. But if everything Bucky said is true, Connor's going to have to learn to accept all this and to protect his little sister while he can.

"Everything," she says, beaming. "I see everything." Her voice is much clearer now. "I see energy everywhere. Around all of you, around me, connecting all of us. I see it in the air. I *feel* it out my window. When it first happened, at David's bar mitzvah, it was overwhelming. It was like seeing everyone's whole lives, but all at once. I knew all the town's secrets, all the ways that some kind of magic worked on the people who live here. I knew it was tied to that strange old woman, Angelina — you know, the one with the birthmark on her cheek in the shape of a duck?"

We laugh. "Yup, we know the one."

Connor isn't laughing, though. "Grace . . . are you sure you're all right? Did you hit your head — is that what caused all this in the first place?"

She turns to me. The power of her gaze is unsettling at first, so different from the little girl of a week ago. I can read her face. She's giving me permission to tell him. I clear my throat. "Um, Grace has these kinds of powers now . . . it's a really long story, but it was something she was born with. Only it didn't come out until she turned ten. There's a lot more to the story, but that's the long and short of it."

Connor looks from me to her. "Is this . . . true?"

Grace nods. She squeezes Connor's hand, and each of us in the room can feel her love and appreciation for him.

"After a few minutes of my head being all jumbled," Grace continues, "everything got quiet. I knew you guys were trying to help me somehow, but I couldn't really focus on any one thing. I heard Angelina in my head. I could still see all these lines, and could sort of figure out how to make them move, like weaving a blanket." She makes the knitting motion to demonstrate. Then stops and stares at her hands. "Hey! Are my hands bigger?"

We laugh again. Connor throws his arms around her. That's the cool thing about him. He bounces back quickly. "Everything's bigger, sis! You grew four inches this week!"

"No way!" she shouts. We all step back so she can get out of bed. "The floor's definitely farther away!" she announces, once she's standing. "Whose pajamas am I wearing?"

"Those would be mine," Rory says. She points to all the clothes hanging in the closet. "Those, too. I'm sorry they aren't, you know, more stylish."

"They're perfect," Grace says.

"Grace," Tara says, approaching the bed. "You said 'but I am' when you first woke up. What did you mean by that?"

Mrs. Kelly rushes back in before Grace can answer. She's carrying a tray with water, an orange, and a bowl of oatmeal. "The doctor's on his way over. He said to start off small, with a few bites." Her eyes spill over again. "Look at you, standing up! My baby's so tall!"

Leo reaches for the tray and catches it right in time. Mrs.

Kelly pulls Grace into her arms. Rory waves the rest of us over to the door. "I think we should leave them."

Connor shakes his head. "One of you has to stay to explain this."

"I'll do it," Tara offers. Even though she's upset with David, it's obvious she wants to honor his request to help out Connor in any way possible.

I squeeze her arm and whisper, "You're the best."

Grace peeks around her mom's shoulder and waves goodbye. "I'll see you guys this afternoon," she says. "At the train station."

"Huh?" the four of us reply at the same time.

She just smiles. Tara's phone dings and she reaches into her pocket for it. She reads the text and when she looks up, her eyes are bright. "David's coming home today. His train gets in at five."

We all turn to look at Grace, who smiles sheepishly. "Oh, boy," Connor says. "So this is how it's going to be from now on. And I thought she was impossible to live with before!"

Mrs. Kelly looks confused.

"I'll explain everything, Mrs. Kelly," Tara says. "Or at least I'll try."

"How about come back in twenty minutes or so?" Mrs. Kelly suggests. "Let me try to get some food in her."

Tara nods and we all give Grace one more hug before heading downstairs. It hits me that our job is done. All that's left is for me and Leo to toast to our friendship, and the curse will be broken. Again.

Leo pulls me aside when we reach the porch. "Hey, what if we don't do that toast? You think we'd still be able to go into the past whenever we want?"

"I don't know. Probably. I'm not sure I want to, though. Maybe Bucky was right. Maybe those ghosts should stay sleeping. They've had their turn."

He squeezes my hand. "I agree."

Tara and Rory join us, and a lump forms in my throat when I see their happy faces. I swallow and say, "I just want to thank you guys for everything you did for me and Leo this week. It's just so above and beyond the call of friendship and I'm so lucky to have you guys and . . . and I'll never forget it."

"Ditto what she said," Leo adds.

Rory and Tara start crying and soon we're all crying, except Leo, who *might* be crying, but he has his head down so it's hard to tell.

"We better get home," I say after a few minutes of going over what Tara's going to say to the Kellys. "You'll let us know how David is, right, Tara? When you meet him at the train?"

"What do you mean? You guys will totally be there."

"Don't you want to see David alone?" I ask, surprised.

She shakes her head. "He'll be with his mom, so it's not going to be this big, private reunion or anything. He didn't even really ask me to come; he just said the train gets in at five, that's all."

"He definitely wants you to come," I assure her.

Ray steps out from the car. "I'll pick you up at four thirty, young lady," he says firmly. "Now go in there and do your best to convince that family that their daughter isn't crazy." I thought he'd been sleeping in there, but apparently he'd heard everything. Tara grins and runs back into the house.

"That thank-you extends to you, too, Ray," I tell him. "You were totally aces!"

"The expression is *ace*," he says, rolling his eyes. "Not *aces*."

"That doesn't sound right."

He groans. "Never mind. Let's get you all home and into the showers."

"Are you saying we smell?" Rory asks as we climb into the car.

"I ain't saying ya don't."

·   ·   ·   ·   ·   ·   ·   ·   ·   ·   ·   ·

When a car honks in my driveway at four thirty, it's Tara's mom, not Ray, behind the wheel of the SUV.

"Is that one of the T-shirts your aunt got you?" I ask Tara as I join Rory and Leo in the back. "I've never seen you in yellow."

"Aunt Bethany told me I have to look cheery when picking up a friend who just spent a week visiting his sick father. Apparently none of my own clothes are cheery. I feel like the surface of the sun."

I lean forward and pat her shoulder. "You do look very sunny. But in a cheery kind of way."

"Now that you're all here," her mom says as we head down the street, "I wanted to ask if your involvement with Angelina is over."

"Yes," Tara replies quickly.

"Hopefully," Rory says.

"Not sure," I say.

"Is anything really over when Angelina is involved?" Leo asks.

Mrs. Brennan sighs. "Well, that clears it up."

To change the subject, Tara tells us all about the house they'll be moving into in a few weeks. "It's right down the street from my aunt and uncle, and it's two floors, and I'll have to sign up for school. Maybe we'll be in the same classes!"

Her mother smiles as she drives, clearly enjoying Tara's excitement. We're halfway to the train station when she says, "Oh, Tara, I almost forgot. A letter came for you today. It's in my pocketbook if you want to grab it."

"A letter?" Tara asks. "Is it from Mrs. Schafer, my English teacher? Or I should say, my old English teacher?"

"Nope."

Tara digs around her mom's large bag until she finds it. "Oh!" she says, staring at the return address written on the back of the envelope.

"Is it from David?" Rory asks, leaning forward.

Tara shakes her head. It takes a full minute before she says, "It's from an old pen pal of mine, Julie." Her voice is really tight when she says it.

"Cool," Rory says. "When was the last time you heard from her?"

Tara hesitates, then says, "Fourth grade." She turns the envelope over and runs her finger over the stamp, which for some reason is on upside down.

"Wow," Rory says. "You've been writing to each other ever since then?"

"Well . . . she wrote for a while. And then we lost touch."

"As I recall, you never wrote her back," her mother says.

"I did, too," Tara argues. "Lots of times. She just didn't receive them until now."

"What do you mean?" I ask.

But Tara doesn't answer.

"Aren't you gonna open it?" Leo asks.

Tara looks at the letter a little longer, then shakes her head and puts it in her pocket. Every few minutes she touches that pocket like she can't quite believe the letter's there.

The parking lot at the train station is pretty empty, as usual. Not too many people come or go from River Bend or Willow Falls or any of the other small towns nearby that this station serves. There are only two tracks, one going south, one north. David and his mom will be arriving on the southbound track. The Kellys' car pulls in right after us, so we wait for them to park before heading over to the platform. Connor and Grace are laughing as they step out into the parking lot. I'm struck again by how Grace has changed. It's not only that she looks older, but she looks wiser, too. Last week she was a little girl, and now, well, she's something else entirely.

Tara's mom hangs back to talk to Mr. and Mrs. Kelly while the rest of us hurry up to the platform. When we're away from all the grown-ups, Grace takes my hand and reaches over for Leo's, too. "You used those chalkboards for a whole year for me! Tara told me about the birthday parties. I knew you guys were trying to help me but I had no idea how far you went. I mean, you went really *far*!"

"Yup," I say. "You were especially cute at four."

She squeezes both our hands and looks us directly in the eye. "Thank you both so much for everything." She says it with such sincerity that I feel her gratitude all the way down to my toes. "Thank you for going back, and thank you for refusing to go back once you learned what was at stake." She squeezes our hands one more time and then moves them closer until somehow Leo and I are left holding hands. She gives a satisfied smile and turns away.

Leo and I don't look at each other, but I can sense his grin anyway.

"We agreed it was best not to tell anyone else about Grace's powers," Connor tells us. "Not right away, at least."

"We won't, either," I promise. "We've learned that until someone has an experience with Angelina, or seen the magic themself, you just wind up sounding crazy."

Tara keeps looking over at the clock on the brick wall. "Five more minutes," she says, shifting her weight from foot to foot.

"The train's going to be early," Grace says.

"Wow, you really are connected to everything!" Tara says. "How do you know that?"

Grace laughs. "Because I can see it coming down the track!"

Tara turns around to see the train coming toward us. "Oh!"

We try not to laugh at Tara, but it comes out anyway. The train pulls up and the doors whoosh open. The only person who steps out is a teenager with a duffel bag. He heads down the platform, whistling. We look up and down the length of the train, craning our necks to see around the bend. Just when I'm about to suggest that maybe they missed the train, David's mom comes into view a few doors down. She steps onto the platform and we all run toward her. David steps out next, carrying two big suitcases. I flash back for a second to the eight-year-old David that we saw a few days ago. He's still there, inside this bigger one. He quickly scans the group and when his eyes land on Tara, his face lights up. He drops the suitcases and runs up to her.

"Hi!" he shouts over the engine noises.

"Hi!" Tara replies, her voice a little shaky. She gives an awkward wave to David's mom. Another two people exit from the last door on the train, and one more man steps off behind David. We step back to let him pass. To my surprise, the man stops.

David takes a deep breath. "Everyone, I'd like you to meet my dad."

Chapter Twenty-Six

We all stare, jaws open, at the man before us. I try to take it in. He is of medium height, wearing glasses, a football jersey, jeans, and sneakers. He has a newspaper tucked under one arm, and a laptop bag on his shoulder. Fit and rosy cheeked, he looks like the complete opposite of someone who has been lying in a bed for the past five years. "Hi, kids," he says. "I've heard a lot about you."

None of us is capable of movement or speech. "Dad, this is Tara, my . . ." He pauses and looks to Tara for confirmation before finishing his sentence. She comes out of her shock enough to nod. "Girlfriend," he finishes with a grin.

"Hello, girlfriend Tara," his father says, patting Tara on the shoulder. "You've made my son very happy."

"Dad!" David says, blushing like this is a normal event, just a son introducing his girlfriend to his father.

Tara chokes out, "It's so great to meet you!" and then resumes her staring, like the rest of us. Even footfalls pounding on the platform behind us can't make us turn away.

"Phil!" a man's voice shouts. Seconds later Mr. Kelly comes barreling past us. "Is it really you?"

David's father (!!!) laughs and puts out his hand. Mr. Kelly embraces him instead, then pulls away. "I'm sorry! I hope I didn't hurt you!"

He laughs again. "No, no, I'm quite hardy now." He flexes his arm to prove it, and they laugh some more.

The train doors swoosh closed, a clear message that we, like that train, can only go forward. One long belch of steam, and it chugs away from the station.

Connor is still staring at David's dad. "What . . . how . . . what . . ." he stutters.

"It's a miracle," David says, his eyes shining the same way they did when he sang during his service. "When we got to the clinic this morning, he was laying in his bed as usual. One of his nurses was in there, rearranging his pillows, then she left. A few minutes later, he blinked, sat up in bed, and said, 'Hi, family, I'm back.'"

"But . . . how?" Rory asks. Next to Connor, she was the one who knew David the best, and knew what he'd gone through with his dad so sick.

"The doctors have no idea. They wanted to keep him there for observation but he was like, 'No way, I'm going home!'"

Rory steps forward to introduce herself and when she moves, Grace comes into view behind her. She's the only one who doesn't look shocked. In fact, she looks kind of like the Cheshire Cat in *Alice in Wonderland*, with a knowing, satisfied smile. Leo spots it, too. I have a feeling we're thinking exactly the same thing. Leo pulls David aside. Tara and I follow. "Your father's nurse," he whispers hurriedly. "What did she look like?"

"Pretty ordinary looking. White hair, short, nurselike. Why?"

"Did she have a duck-shaped birthmark on her cheek?" I ask.

"No, I don't think so. Wait, you mean like that old lady in town?"

"Yes, like her," I reply.

"I'm sure I would have noticed that," he says.

"Did she wear a lot of makeup?" Tara asks in a hushed voice.

"I can't say I know a lot about makeup. But I guess she did. It can't be the same person you're thinking of, though. This lady is a *nurse*. And it's not like she had anything to do with my dad's recovery. She's been coming to see him ever since he was a little kid. If she could've fixed him, she'd have done it a long time ago." He keeps glancing over at his dad, as though he's afraid he'll suddenly vanish.

Leo and Tara and I stare at one another, then back at David. "How long ago did they meet, exactly?"

He thinks back. "Maybe thirty-five years ago or something? My dad was around five. He was having these occasional spasms and his parents had heard about this clinic, the same one we just came from. On the way to get my dad checked out, they decided to stop in Willow Falls for lunch because they wanted to show my dad where his great-grandfather had been born." He turns around. "Hey, Dad, where did you guys go when you stopped in Willow Falls that one time when you were a kid?"

"Some kind of diner, I think. They had the best chocolate chip pancakes! Mmm . . . pancakes!" He rubs his belly. "I can't wait to eat pancakes again after almost a decade of protein drinks!"

And then all at once, I understand. I can tell from Leo's and Tara's faces that they do, too. Angelina had been trying for thirty-five years to fix David's dad because she couldn't fix his great-grandfather Joshua! If she had been able to cure him, then David's dad — and David himself — wouldn't have inherited the disease. I repeat Angelina's last words to us: "I'm still not strong enough."

"But I am," Tara says, imitating Grace's first words upon waking.

I get the chills when she says it.

"What are you guys talking about?" David asks.

"Where is she?" Tara says, turning in a circle. "Where's Grace?"

Mr. and Mrs. Kelly realize she's missing, too, and start to panic, running up and down the platform, checking behind the benches.

"There!" Rory shouts, pointing across the tracks to the northbound platform.

Grace, her red hair gleaming in the sun, stands beside an old couple, one very short, one very tall, both with very white hair. The man has two large suitcases at his feet. The woman carries a cane with the handle in the shape of a duck. It's impossible to equate her with the eighteen-year-old girl we met last night.

"Look who's finally come back to town," Leo says. Tara's mother narrows her eyes and looks as if she'd like to go bounding over there to give Angelina a piece of her mind. Something tells me Mrs. Brennan isn't quite as forgiving of Angelina's methods as we've been. Tara puts her hand firmly on her mom's arm.

They are too far away for us to make out their words. We watch as Grace and Angelina both nod, then embrace. Angelina's never been a hugger, but I suppose for the girl who is finally freeing her of her self-imposed century-long penance, she can squeeze out one hug. The whistle blows, announcing the arrival of the next train. Grace pulls away, then goes to hug Bucky. Finally she heads toward the stairwell that connects the platforms, clutching what looks from here to be a regular old shoe box. Angelina and Bucky turn toward the track in preparation to board the approaching train. David does a double take, then exclaims, "Hey, there's my dad's nurse! She must have been on our train. I wonder where she's going?"

In another few seconds we won't be able to see them. Just before the train pulls into the station and hides them from view, Bucky looks right at Leo and me. "Thank you," he mouths.

We nod in response and wave. I don't expect a thank-you from Angelina, and we don't get one. But as the train pulls away with them on it, she presses her face to the window nearest us and winks. That's good enough for me.

Epilogue
Grace

Our parents are helping the Goldbergs take their bags to their car, so we climb into Dad's backseat to wait. "That's it?" Connor asks, pointing to the present Angelina gave me. "A hundred years of wisdom inside a shoe box?"

"I'm sure it's not *just* a shoe box," I argue, feeling the need to defend her. "Angelina works in mysterious ways, remember?"

"Maybe it's a *magical* shoe box," he says. "Now you can make the footwear of your dreams appear inside with a tap of your finger. Or is it a twitch of your nose? How *are* you supposed to make stuff happen anyway?"

"I really don't —"

"Hey," he interrupts. "What number am I thinking of? Who's gonna win the World Series this year? When school starts will you make it so I have four gym periods every day and no math? And make it so all the girls on the gymnastics team fight over me and . . ."

"I'm so glad you're not going to treat me any differently," I say, pinching him on the leg.

"Sorry," he says sheepishly. "You're right. Just one girl on the gymnastics team will be fine."

I laugh. "I'm glad you're my brother."

"And I'm glad you're the chosen one and not me. All that helping people would take away from my video game time."

We get quiet as our parents climb in the front seats, full of talk of the miracle of Mr. Goldberg's recovery. Mom keeps glancing at me in the rearview mirror like she wants to ask me something but isn't sure she wants to know the answer. Part of me wishes my parents didn't know about what's happening to me. They're going to want to try to protect me and shelter me and make it easier, and I don't think they'll be able to do that.

Even if I wanted to, I can't do any of the stuff Connor asked of me, at least not for two more years. Curing David's dad took the last of Angelina's powers and most of mine, too. Angelina told me it will take two years to fully replenish them. Even though I won't be able to control much, I can still sense the stream of time and I can see the web that connects everyone to everyone else. I'm kind of glad for the time off. Starting middle school next year will be hard enough.

I look around the car, curious what the energy will tell me. My family's thoughts come quickly and easily. Connor wants me to open the box. My mother's thoughts come like lightning. She is wired like she's been shot through with electricity. One second she's thinking that if her daughter is some kind of vortex of power, what are her duties as the vortex's mother? Is there a job description on the Internet? Then she decides that she'll have to get me a cell phone now so she can keep track of me while I'm off doing vortex business. (Bonus!)

Dad just wants coffee.

Angelina told me she'll teach me how to shut my mind to all the voices, but I've mostly figured it out. I figured out a lot during that week of silence. You learn a lot more from listening than talking. I did not know this, before.

The shoe box rests much too lightly on my lap to hold a pair of shoes. It almost feels empty. Contrary to what Connor thinks, I can't tell what's inside. "All right," I reply to his unasked question, and lift the lid. He leans over and frowns down at a carefully folded train schedule covered in small blue ink. Below it, the corner of a small, square, yellowed envelope peeks out. "Bummer," he says. "Not a pair of high tops." He settles back and leaves me to it.

I start with the train schedule. I find the words *Dearest Grace* in one corner and begin there, turning the paper in circles as I follow the words.

I am writing this the old-fashioned way, with ink on paper on a moving train. I must start off with an apology, and they do not come easy for me. I was not ready to share my secrets, to show you (or anyone) the threads that bind this town. I am sorry to have frightened your family this past week, but I had to protect you, and them. You were spilling secrets without knowing it, telling tales that weren't yours to tell. People would have figured it out, had they heard more. You are so young to carry this burden, this highest responsibility. I do not recall feeling as young when it was my turn, although no doubt my mother felt differently.

My life has been filled every day with equal parts beauty and sadness, regret and joy. So I silenced you to borrow some time, to give Amanda and Leo a chance to do what I couldn't achieve the first time. But you have surprised me, young Grace. You were not frightened by what you saw, these weavings of time and place. You held tight to your connection with it, as I suppose I did as well, so long ago. There is not room for both of us, not for long. The old must always make way for the young; time goes only in one direction for a reason. It is your turn, Grace.

Amanda and Leo, Rory, and Tara, they have taken up residence in this old lady's heart, although they may be surprised to hear of it. And David, well, it was all about him in the end, wasn't it? You have a larger family now. They, and I, will be here for you. You will not be alone as you enter this new world. When you are eighteen, you will find your own way, as it was for me, and for those who came before.

Think of the moments with your loved ones as gifts, presents for the years when those around you have run out of birthdays, but you have not. I have one last present for you, which you will find in this box. It will open doors to wonders unimagined. Use it or don't.

Take the next two years to learn and grow. You will be older by the time your full strength is restored, and more prepared to take on the life you were chosen for. I will visit, will tend my herb garden, will watch the trees of Apple Grove grow tall enough to once again provide shade for the townspeople to dance under. You can always find me if you need me. Well, not always, I suppose. Now that my power has been spent, my long life will one day catch up with me. But let us not dwell in dark places. It is much nicer to walk in the light. The present — the here and now — is perhaps the greatest gift.

I shall be leaving town for a while, a few months, even. There is much I have not seen of the world outside our little town, and as the saying goes, there is no time like the present. If you run into Bucky Whitehead, tell him he's the most charming fiddler I ever did see.

Angelina

I reread the letter, smiling at the line about Bucky. I had been worried that alerting him earlier to her arrival may have been a mistake. I knew she loved him, and he her, but I've never played matchmaker before. Turned out that he'd had their suitcases packed since my birthday.

I pick up the envelope, feeling the outline of the hard, key-shaped object inside. I try to sense the lock's location, but Angelina must have blocked it. I wonder what else she has shielded from me. I will trust, for now, that she is still looking out for my best interests. Flipping the envelope over reveals two words: *Ask Tara.*

·　·　·　·　·　·　·　·　·　·　·

"It's down here?" I ask, craning my neck to see down the narrow alley. "I've never been here before. Aren't these stores closed down?"

Tara and the other girls exchange smiles. "Only sometimes," Tara says. She leads the way while David, Leo, and Connor trail behind to distance themselves from anything that has to do with shopping. David is talking nonstop about his father and the plans they made on the train for the rest of the summer, and how now his mom won't be so sad all the time and maybe they'll get a dog. It has not yet occurred to him that he no longer has to worry about when the disease will strike him. This realization will come soon, tonight after dinner. Tara will be the first person he tells, Connor the second. Not paying attention, David stumbles on the uneven cobblestones, pitching forward. A tiny flick of my hand and he's upright again, only partially aware he almost fell. I'm pretty handy to have around!

I glance at the stores as we pass by. They don't look like much fun. A whole store for watches? A sign in the barbershop window promises a shave and a haircut for two dollars. Sure, maybe fifty years ago. "Are you sure my key has something to do with these stores?"

Tara stops in front of the last store. "Just this one." The letters on the top of the door spell out ANGELINA'S SWEET REPEATS AND COLLECTIBLES. Angelina left me a key to a thrift shop? The girls use their forearms to sweep away circles of dust from the large glass windows lining the storefront. I can now clearly see the contents of the store, stuff stacked high on shelves, hung on racks, piled in corners. Even from this distance, I can see the objects glowing with their history. I can see who owned them, and I can see why the owners brought them here to sell. I can see who needs them. Sorting through all these things will take years. Maybe that's what Angelina had in mind.

David steps forward, pressing his face to the glass. "Hey! When did all that stuff get here?"

"Finally!" Tara shouts as the others burst out laughing. She runs up to David and he faces her, his eyes wide with surprise. We all turn away.

It's not polite to watch someone's first kiss.

Wendy Mass is the author of award-winning books for young readers, including *11 Birthdays, Finally, 13 Gifts,* and the Twice Upon a Time series: *Rapunzel, The One with All the Hair; Sleeping Beauty, The One Who Took the Really Long Nap;* and *Beauty and the Beast, The Only One Who Didn't Run Away;* as well as *A Mango-Shaped Space, Jeremy Fink and the Meaning of Life, Heaven Looks a Lot Like the Mall, Leap Day, Every Soul a Star,* and *The Candymakers.* She lives with her family in New Jersey.

Wendy Mass's birthday books are like a wish come true!